Mary A. M. Marks

All the World's a Stage

A novel. Part 2

Mary A. M. Marks

All the World's a Stage
A novel. Part 2

ISBN/EAN: 9783337051204

Printed in Europe, USA, Canada, Australia, Japan

Cover: Foto ©Andreas Hilbeck / pixelio.de

More available books at **www.hansebooks.com**

ALL THE WORLD'S A STAGE.

A Novel.

BY

MARY A. M. HOPPUS.

Some men's sins
go beforehand to
judgment, and
some follow after.

IN THREE VOLUMES.
VOL. II.

LONDON:

SAMPSON LOW, MARSTON, SEARLE & RIVINGTON,

CROWN BUILDINGS, 188, FLEET STREET.

1879.

LONDON:
PRINTED BY WILLIAM CLOWES AND SONS,
STAMFORD STREET AND CHARING CROSS.

ALL THE WORLD'S A STAGE.

CHAPTER I.

A young and learned doctor.
Merchant of Venice.

MRS. FIREBRACE had not found it difficult to induce Charlotte to come back with her to Queen Anne Street when the autumn damps drove them from Twickenham. Russell Square would be very lonely, and what society could Charlotte see there now?

It had been settled from the very first that they were all to go down to Dockhampton for Christmas, and neither of the girls thought of much else as the time drew near. The Overtons were all in London, with the exception of

Gerald, who had accepted the post refused by Theodore Paston. Sir Saville and Lady Fidelle had taken a house looking on the Green Park.

At an evening party in South Audley Street Charlotte met Mr. Vincent for the first time since her refusal of him. He was so busy explaining some prints to Amelia, that he did not see Charlotte until she was quite near. He rose instantly, and after a polite inquiry or two offered her his chair, and, taking another for himself, entertained both the ladies till some one began to sing. Charlotte thought him changed. Was he looking a little older, a little stouter, and yet a little more worn, than when she last saw him? She could not tell; but the dusky flush which alone had betrayed his emotion on meeting her was long in subsiding, and the cast in his eye was certainly very noticeable.

As soon as the song was over, Lady Overton called Mr. Vincent away, and Charlotte involuntarily said—

" You have seen a great deal of Mr. Vincent lately ? "

" Yes ; papa likes him extremely. What a delightful talker he is !—at least, mamma thinks so."

Again as it seemed in spite of herself, Charlotte said, " Don't you ? "

" Oh yes—of course. Nobody could help thinking so," said Amelia, the colour spreading from her cheeks to her chin, and then up to her soft smooth hair.

Charlotte had never loved Mr. Vincent, as we know ; but she was exceedingly sharp-sighted where he was concerned. What would Lady Overton say? Charlotte began to wonder whether Mr. Vincent would run away with Amelia, as Mr. Paston's father had with Diana Gifford. She bade him good night quite cordially ; and, as she sat with Adelaide over her bedroom fire, astonished her cousin by suddenly bursting out with—

" Adelaide, I'm half inclined to think I have wronged Mr. Vincent ! "

" Wronged him, dear ?   How ? "

" Why, I've always suspected him ever since dear papa took him out of his will, and wrote that letter to me, about having no proofs ; and now I am almost beginning to believe that perhaps the letter had nothing to do with Mr. Vincent after all."

" What did you suspect him of ? "

"I don't know.   It would be dreadful if I had wronged him all the time."

" You did not wish to wrong him, Charlotte dear."

" I'm afraid I did.   I never liked him.   I think I was a little jealous.   I'm afraid I have been awfully wicked."

Charlotte's self-reproach led her to take a greater interest in the fate of Amelia than she might otherwise have done—that young lady having hitherto bored her considerably. No hint reached her of any love-making, but Lina told her one day that Mr. Counsellor Bingham and Mr. Vincent were going to try and put an end to the law-suit which had been

worrying papa for years, and that Mr. Bingham thought Mr. Vincent had discovered something which would decide the case in their
favour.

CHAPTER II.

Angels are painted fair, to look like you.
Venice Preserved.

HORACE had taken lodgings for his expected
guests in a pleasant little house, on the London
Road. Here the coach set down Mrs. Firebrace,
Charlotte, and Adelaide, early on a rainy
December evening, and here a little later
Horace came to them from the theatre. It
was an "off night," but preparations for the
Christmas piece were now being pushed forward rapidly, and every one was busy. In fact,
as Horace went on to tell the ladies, he had
left Mr. Kiddle hard at work superintending
the carpenter, and had promised to return in
an hour.

"Dear me! how intensely interesting!" exclaimed Sophia. "And what is the carpenter doing, if it is not an indiscreet question?"

"Not at all. He is just now engaged upon the Magic Cave," said Horace smiling. "Mr. Kiddle expects it to be very effective. When the Enchanted Rocks (they are finished, but of course not set up) are struck by the Fairy Prince, a hollow groan is heard—— "

"How intensely romantic!" exclaimed Sophia.

"And a portion of the rock, giving way, discloses a cavern."

"Charming!" said Sophia.

"At the other end of which an exquisite garden is perceived; then—— "

"Pray pardon me," said Theodore Paston (who had been waiting to receive the ladies when they alighted from the coach, and had been—by Charlotte—invited to remain to tea). "Do not reveal the plan to the ladies—they will lose the surprise, which is a great part of the secret of art."

"Indeed, Paston? I'm glad to hear you

say so," said Horace eagerly. " 'Twas but
the other day you were maintaining that art
was not a succession of surprises, but the
steady and visible approach of an inevitable
catastrophe."

"So it is—in *Hamlet*," said Theodore,
" and so it is not, in this Fairy Extravaganza
which you are putting on the boards. There
is a place for surprises, and a place for what is
foreseen."

" Now, really, Mr. Paston, you are too bad !
You allow our curiosity to be excited, and
then you won't suffer it to be satisfied."

Sophia shook her curls engagingly at
Theodore, with an air which seemed to say,
" I am naturally dying to know, but I have
not the slightest desire to peep unlawfully."
After which she added, " I had a favour to
ask, but Mr. Paston has made me afraid."

" I deserve pardon. I spoke in the interest
of the extravaganza," exclaimed Theodore with
a mock-penitent gesture acquired at Vogelheimsburg.

" Well, cousin Horace has only to say it's not the proper thing, and of course we shall think no more about it; but we all did say, coming along in the coach—and oh, my dear cousin, if you had but heard an old gentleman who got out at Basingstoke going on about the railway works that they've begun at Nine Elms—but, as I was saying, we all said how romantic it would be, if cousin Horace would take us behind the scenes, and let us see what it is all like——"

"Do not look at me so imploringly, Mrs. Firebrace," said Mr. Paston laughing, "as though I were going to raise an objection. There is no reason at all why you should not go ; is there, Mr. Lancaster ?"

" None at all. It has left off raining for some time, and is now starlight," said Horace.

This conversation was a great deal longer than appears here, and it was by no means confined to theatrical matters. Horace seemed to have forgotten all about Mr. Kiddle anxiously expecting him to return and decide

how the Prince should approach the Enchanted
Palace—whether by the Avenue of Magnolias,
or through the Garden of Roses, both of which
localities were casually mentioned by the
Prince in his speech on entering the enchanted
ground.   It was Charlotte who at last suggested that perhaps they had better go at
once.

When the ladies, piloted by Horace, and
lighted by Theodore—who carried a patri-
archal lantern borrowed from the landlady—
had safely made their way over the half-dry
pavements, and arrived at the stage door of
the theatre, it soon became apparent that Mr.
Kiddle had gone home, tired of waiting, and
probably aware by this time that Mr. Lancaster
occasionally forgot what o'clock it was.

"The door is locked," said Mr. Paston, who
as linkman was a step or two in advance.

"Ah, I dare say Kiddle thought I should
not be able to get away in time," observed
Horace carelessly.   "It is no matter; I have
a key.   Take my arm up the stairs, Sophia."

"No, thank you, cousin," said Sophia, briskly. " I am not in the least tired. Take Addy; she needs an arm much more than I do, poor child. She has been looking *so* pale lately."

Thanks to her mother's adroitness, Adelaide found herself delivered over to Horace's exclusive care. Mr. Paston, thus circumvented at the outset of the new campaign, fumed, and offering his arm to Miss Lancaster let Mrs. Firebrace trip up the stairs alone.

" Are you cold, Adelaide ? " asked Horace, feeling the girl tremble.

" No, not exactly cold ; but it is so ghostly," said Adelaide.

They had found their way (very indifferently lighted by Theodore) to the manager's own sanctum—if such a word may be applied to an imperfectly partitioned closet, choked with chests containing dresses and properties, and littered with all sorts of theatrical material, from a pen to a powder-puff, from a looking-glass to a tea-kettle. From this chaotic lumber-room, as it seemed to the ladies,

Horace led them (having found and lighted a couple of wax-candles) through other and larger lumber-rooms, one of which he said was the carpenter's shop, and which was crammed with, among innumerable more familiar objects, what seemed to be the disjointed sections of a colossal dissecting-puzzle. A very large room beyond this, which wandered off round its own corners into apparently illimitable darknesses, was lined many times deep with more of these dissecting-puzzles.

Sophia thought it all seemed very dingy and dirty, so she said, " What an interesting place ! " and narrowly avoided falling down an awkward step which she had not observed.

" This is the scenery for a good many plays," said Horace, holding his candle so near that he dropped some wax on the pinnacle of a church in Cyprus. " I am afraid you will despise our poor painted shows, now you have seen them so near."

" It is not the scenery that is the best part --it is the acting," said Adelaide, who, what with cold, fatigue, and excitement, was quivering from head to foot.

"Would you like to see what the stage is like?" asked Horace. "Take care—there is a step, and here are three more. Now we are coming to what we call 'the wings.'"

Clinging to Horace's arm, Adelaide peered into the darkness, which the solitary candle only made visible. The dingy curtain might have been let down from heaven itself for anything they could see of its origin.

"It will all look very different to-morrow night," said Horace. "It will be as it were transformed."

"What is the piece?" asked Adelaide timidly. She was deeply impressed with the weirdness and strangeness of the place, and with the thought that it was the magic of Horace's genius which would transform it all to-morrow.

"We are playing *Venice Preserved*; and as soon as the Christmas holidays are over, I intend to bring out *Damon and Pythias*."

"How strange it all is! How awful it would be to be shut up here alone!" exclaimed Adelaide, but very softly. She could not speak loud in that strange place, which seemed to have neither roof nor walls, and yet to be full of chambers and corridors. "If there are any ghosts, I think they must feel as I do to-night."

As she spoke, Horace was for the first time really struck by that resemblance to the portrait of his ancestress, which Theodore Paston had so often remarked upon. Adelaide's expression struck him altogether. She was dressed in a travelling pelisse of some soft grey stuff; and instead of a bonnet she had put on to-night a hood of the same material, which had slightly fallen back, and showed to great advantage the fine oval of her face, and her rich dark hair. Horace compared her regretfully with Mrs. Kiddle, who could never be made to look like *Belvidera*, even in the splendid black lace veil which he had very grudgingly lent her in sheer despair.

"You would confer a great favour on me, Adelaide," he said, "if you would take this candle, and move slowly across the stage. I wish to study an effect for *Belvidera*."

Adelaide took the candle, and was stepping beyond the shelter of the wings, when another light was seen approaching, and Sophia's vivacious voice and laugh broke the silence.

"Here you are, I do declare!" cried Sophia. "Why, Addy, what are you going to do?"

Horace explained that he was far from satisfied with Mrs. Kiddle's *Belvidera*, and hoped to get a hint for improving her from Adelaide, "who looks the part to perfection. I wonder I never observed it before," he added to Theodore, who replied—

"She could do more than look the part, as I have often said to you. But let me fetch the veil. Mrs. Kiddle wears it like a gipsy's shawl. We will learn from Miss Grant how a Venetian dame should wear it."

Theodore hastened away, and very quickly

returned with the veil thrown over his shoulder, and two more candles, which he lighted, and stuck in frightfully precarious parts of the scenery. Meantime, Mrs. Fire-brace—who for once was grateful to Mr. Paston—had insisted that Addy should slip off her pelisse, which was too heavy to be consistent with "a real Italian veil."

"And I'm sure I never felt such lace in my life," said Sophia, as she arranged it over Adelaide's black gown, and gave a final touch to the folds which fell on either side her head. "Where *did* you get it, cousin Horace?"

"It belonged to the original of the picture which Adelaide resembles," said Horace, looking with much approval on the result of Sophia's manipulations. "She wore it in several of her parts. I consider it desecrated by Mrs. Kiddle, but it was the only thing that made her endurable. I cannot play *Jaffier* to a woman who looks like Black-Eyed Susan!"

Adelaide's plain black gown seemed to have undergone a transformation—all of it, at least, which could be seen through the soft ample folds of the veil. As she glided over the stage, candle in hand, her figure seemed, even in the uncertain light, to acquire a tragic grandeur ; and her face, when she turned and came towards the little group at the wings, might have served as a model for a painter who wished to represent *Belvidera* before she yet knows her husband's guilt. Adelaide was not at all embarrassed ; she was too well used to hear of theatrical matters, and too unaffectedly glad to think she could serve Horace, to be self-conscious.

"Thank you a thousand times," he said, when he had made her stand in various attitudes, and had said at each new change, "Mrs. Kiddle must and shall do as I tell her in future. See, Paston, it *is* possible to avoid looking like a fortune-teller. I'll stop the piece if she is obstinate !"

"Miss Grant would be an admirable *Belvidera*," said Mr. Paston, who had never taken his eyes off her.

"She is splendid!" said Charlotte. "Isn't she, Horry dear?"

"'Angels are painted fair, to look like you.'"

Horace should not have said this so loud, and with so much feeling. Adelaide heard him, and turned first very pale, and then very red, and instantly began to take off the veil and put on her pelisse, which Mr. Paston had been holding.

That line out of his own part in *Venice Preserved* seemed to run in Horace's head to-night. Theodore heard him murmuring it to himself more than once as they went home after seeing the ladies to their lodgings.

CHAPTER III.

Polonius. Look, whether he has not turn'd his colour,
and has tears in 's eyes.

ADELAIDE found it very difficult to realize that
the splendour and impressiveness of *Venice
Preserved* owed anything to the dreary and
dusty chaos through which she had wandered
last night. She did not despise the lath-and-
canvas streets, as Horace had said he feared
she would; only shallow and vulgar natures
can be disillusioned thus. She was all the more
impressed by the reality, because she knew
that it was clad in unreality. There are persons who speak as though they were proud to
own that a pasteboard palace is to them a
pasteboard palace; and that they are so much
alive to the incongruities of the stage, that

they derive little if any edification from the tragedy. These persons are correct in their judgment as far as they go ; everything which appeals to the senses must be shown *somehow,* that is, it must be shown in some one particular way, to the exclusion of other ways. And dramatic art has, like all other arts, its own particular limitations. But these persons should go a little farther. If they had the courage of their opinions, they would probably confess that to them a picture too is a puerile deception, which never imposes upon them sufficiently to cause them the slightest emotion. After all, how utterly unreal is a picture ! The frame alone ought to disillusion a clear-headed person once and for all. Do we behold real landscapes, real persons and actions, enclosed within the narrow limits of a gilded frame, and hung on a wall ? But not every one has eyes keen enough to discern the canvas through the Rafaele, and confess that all is vanity.

This part of *Jaffier* was the first Adelaide had ever seen her cousin in, and she never

quite ceased to identify him with it. To
identify the buxom Mrs. Kiddle with *Belvidera* was less easy. (Adelaide had read the
acting-edition of the play, that afternoon.)
Venice Preserved is a singular instance of
great merit combined with enormous defect.
Had the motive for Jaffier's treason been as
adequate as that for Othello's murder of Des-
demona, we should not feel that we must
apologize to our judgment for the interest
which we take in him. But the play is
so full of beautiful and tender touches, so
many of its lines go straight home, that even
the unreality of the plot cannot make the
characters unreal; and we feel that we are
reading the garbled report of facts which
actually occurred—but not quite thus, rather
than the wild tragedy of a poet whose moral
instincts were less sure than his dramatic
perceptions.

Horace Lancaster's *Jaffier* was one of the
best of his parts—it demanded much to which
he was equal, and little to which he was un-

equal. Charlotte sobbed aloud, without any attempt at concealment; and Adelaide was perhaps still more deeply moved, although she shed only a few very hot tears, which almost scalded her cheeks, but were observed by no one but Charlotte and perhaps by Mr. Paston. Sophia pronounced Mrs. Kiddle "a horrid, vulgar thing, and so fat, too!" Even Adelaide wondered that Horace had not found a more dignified *Belvidera*. The little episode of the night before haunted her memory all through the play, and produced in her a curious confusion of identity, so that when *Jaffier* exclaimed in deep, thrilling tones—

"Angels are painted fair, to look like you,"

she was glad to shrink back behind Charlotte, who sat in the front of the box, and hide the scorching blush which it seemed to her every one must see and wonder at. And yet in the very midst of the blush (so little self-engrossed was Adelaide), she thought of Lady Fidelle, and wondered how she would feel if she heard Horace say that. "But it would be too late now," thought Adelaide, with a sigh which made Sophia turn her head sharply round, and presently make Addy take her seat —"to see better." Sophia meant, *to be seen* better; she was sure that Horace looked very often towards their box, and she thought it a great pity he should not see Addy when he did so.

The feelings of Lady Fidelle seemed to have been a subject for Charlotte's thoughts also this evening. As the girls stood by the fire, after their return to their lodgings, waiting for Mrs. Firebrace, who was still engaged in repairing any little damages which her toilette had received, Charlotte suddenly exclaimed—

"I think Blanche would have been sorry, if she had seen him to-night. Lina doesn't think she gets on very well with Sir Saville; but she never says a word—she'd rather die than tell even Lina. I'm sure she looks ever so much older already, and she hasn't been married three months yet."

CHAPTER IV.

Othello. I know thou 'rt full of love and honesty.

Mr. Vincent came down on Christmas Eve.
Any little awkwardness which Charlotte might
still have felt—especially at meeting him in
her brother's presence—was speedily forgotten
in the news Mr. Vincent brought of the earth-
quake in Leicestershire the day before, which
had frightened the people at Woodhouse Eaves
(a good many of whom were in church at the
time) nearly out of their wits. This, and the
wet journey from town, furnished ample
material for conversation that evening.

Mr. Vincent was a good deal alone with
Horace. His time in Dockhampton was to be
but short, and Horace had many things about

which to consult him. He could not be said
to avoid the ladies, and Theodore Paston was
ready and willing to do duty for both him and
Horace; so that no one (except Mrs. Firebrace)
had any cause to quarrel with the visitor.

The preparations for the Christmas piece had
reached the stage of confusion worse confounded
which usually precedes a new performance.
Mr. Lancaster had realized a good many of
Parnassus Smith's forebodings in the glaring
innovations which he had compelled Kiddle
to adopt. The ballet would be ruined (in the
stage manager's opinion) by the *Louis-Quinze*
costumes on which Mr. Lancaster had insisted. Mr. Kiddle was of course aware
that many pious persons looked on the ballet
with horror, as indecent; but he was quite
unprepared to find a manager looking on it
with disgust, as ugly. Yet this was the
position which Mr. Lancaster took up, and
from which all Kiddle's arguments and en-
treaties failed to dislodge him.

"It is neither graceful nor beautiful," the

manager said. "A troupe of shuttlecocks would be far more pleasing than these ridiculous, short-petticoated, thick-legged women. Those of them who are pretty look a thousand times prettier in the poor and shabby garments they put on to go home in ; and the fat and ugly ones—good heavens ! Kiddle, what would the ancient Greeks have said to a modern ballet girl ?   I blush for my nation, which can enjoy, or imagine that it enjoys, a spectacle which outrages every canon of art, and every law of beauty.   It is a national disgrace !"

"I don't know anything about the ancient Greeks, Mr. Lancaster," replied Kiddle, doggedly, "except that they seem to have gone without their clothes altogether, which I don't suppose you would wish to uphold.   But the Greeks are neither here nor there.   We've got to play to a Dockhampton pit, and a Dockhampton pit won't care a dump for these Louis-what-d'ye-call-him costumes.   And a pretty penny they'll cost us, to begin with."

"That, Mr. Kiddle, is my own affair," said

Horace, in the manner which had provoked his exasperated stage manager to say, that one never knew when Mr. Lancaster was off the boards, and that it was very hard to deal with a man who would turn on you like a book, when you were only talking business, and were not ready with a speech out of a play to answer him with.

On this occasion, Kiddle said rather shortly, " Well, sir, I wish it may succeed ;" and the subject was dropped.

On Christmas Day, they all went to church. Even Mr. Vincent, who was seldom seen at church, was there to-day. It was rather a singular thing that a man so little given to eccentricity or irregularity of any kind should not, if only out of respect for conventional propriety, have conformed to ordinary usage in this matter. But he was consistent with himself. Clear and acute as his intellect was, he never even pretended to any poetical faculty. He judged of art as he judged of all other things, disclaiming the transcen-

dental, and trying everything by the clear light
of intellect. But though he was careful to say
that he did not profess to be a judge of art,
his judgment was invariably correct. If Mr.
Vincent said of a book, "This will please such
and such a class of readers," the event always
justified him; although he frankly admitted
that he himself did not always sufficiently
appreciate many things of whose merits he was
yet aware. He carried the same curious imper-
sonality—if one may so describe the power of
understanding what he did not heartily admire
—into his views on religion. On this very
Christmas morning, Horace had said as they
were at breakfast—

"Dick, I hope you will come to church with
us. It grieves me to feel, as I do sometimes,
that whenever I rise into the highest regions of
human thought and feeling, I must leave you
as it were a little outside. I feel this in my
profession, and whenever we talk of art. Do
not let me feel it in religion."

"My dear fellow," said Vincent, as he

buttered his toast, "I have often said to you, when you have spoken thus, that I make it a rule to attend to what I thoroughly understand, and not to waste my energies upon matters which have no practical bearing on the business of life."

"No practical bearing, Dick? Why, where would morality be, without the sanction of religion?"

"Judging from where it is now, I should think it would be pretty much where it now is," said Vincent quietly. "I am not one of those theorists who attribute all immorality to the ill effects of priestcraft. Most men do, and always will do, as much or as little as they have courage to do; and if the fear of Heaven did not restrain them, the fear of man would. On the other hand, I do not observe that the fear of Heaven prevents men in general from doing what they have a mind to, if they are only clever and bold enough—or even believe themselves to be so, to succeed. For myself, if the actual, tangible dangers of any course of action did not determine me against it, no invisible terrors would move me. I am, I am aware, deficient in imagination" —here Mr. Vincent smiled, and paused an instant to adroitly cut his toast into squares— "but so are most men; and, being so, they fear the unseen less than the seen."

"You speak as though all men did right from fear."

"By no means. Prudence keeps most of them far within the limits where fear need begin to operate."

"How base you must think most men, Dick, to speak thus of them!"

"No; not base. But I cannot help seeing that few men have sufficient resolution or daring to carry out any unusual plan, whether that plan be lawful or unlawful."

"Say legal or illegal, Dick! I believe with you lawyers 'tis much the same."

"How can it be otherwise? All other standards differ with each individual, who thinks everything wrong which he himself has not courage to do, and everything venial at least which he himself dares do."

"Dick, when you speak thus I wonder how we can be the friends we are! Nay; do not look hurt. I know the noble nature which your cynicism covers. But cast the ugly cloak from you—be yourself!"

"My dear Horace, these are my opinions, I assure you. And I do not see how an unprejudiced observer can form any other."

"There are many men whose lives are a direct contradiction to all you have said—men who live for eternity."

"And are therefore all the better thought of in time. When it is proved to me that they could have done better for themselves, all things considered, in any other way, I will think of setting aside the results of my general experience of life."

"And do you never feel the need, or at least the desire, to lean on a higher Power? Does your soul never long to rise above earthly things?"

" Perhaps it might, if it were not obliged to occupy itself in getting a few earthly things. It is easy for you, my dear Horace to talk of despising earthly things—you have a good many of them."

" We shall never understand each other, Dick, on this matter," said Horace with a sigh. " But at least, come with us to church."

" Willingly," said Vincent. " I always intended to do so."

CHAPTER V.

My title's good, and better far than his.
3rd Part of King Henry VI.

THAT was a very curious Christmas Day which Adelaide spent at Dockhampton. They dined at Horace's rooms. It was impossible to drive Princess Paribanou and the Magician out of one's head, or out of one's conversation. Mr. Paston kept up a lively discussion on the overture, and every now and then illustrated his meaning by rushing across the room, seizing his violin, and playing the passage he was referring to. In the interludes of these professional details Mr. Vinçent's affairs were touched on. Adelaide learned that the Overton law-suit was to come on next term. At Mrs.

Firebrace's request (preferred with the laudable
object of keeping Theodore Paston in the
background), Mr. Vincent gave them an out-
line of such of the facts as were generally
known. Keeping to himself the discovery
which, thanks to Sir John's irrepressible
jubilation over his enemy, a good many people
knew that the young barrister had made, Mr.
Vincent put what he did tell so clearly that
Adelaide was able to follow it all with ease,
and wondered why Lina had always said it
was too hard for any but lawyers to understand.

It seemed that nearly a hundred years
before, the Overton of that day had married
an heiress. She was the only daughter of
Lord Hawkesbury, and the title and entailed
estates went to her first cousin, whose great-
grandson died without issue some seven or
eight years since. The late lord was a peculiar
man ; he had quarrelled furiously with the
cousin who was his nearest relative, but had
always maintained very friendly relations with

the Overtons ; and after the quarrel had
spoken of Sir John as his heir—that is, heir
to the estates which had come to his great-
grandfather. On his death, and partly incited
by a grudge of his own against the new
viscount, Sir John had laid an action to
recover the Hawkesbury estates, but had been
non-suited, on the ground that there was no
evidence to show that the deed supposed to
have been executed by the former viscount
had any existence save in the late lord's
imagination.

According to him, when Evelina Hawkesbury married Sir Robert Overton, Lord
Hawkesbury, who was excessively attached to
his daughter, and who was then a widower of
forty-five or fifty, had sent for his nephew and
heir-presumptive, and informed him that he had
always intended on his daughter's marriage
to marry again himself, but was ready to
promise not to do so, if his nephew would join
him in changing the entail. The change Lord
Hawkesbury had proposed was to provide that

all the entailed estates should, in the event of
failure of the direct male line, revert to the
eldest male descendant of his daughter's marriage. To this somewhat singular proposition
the nephew had consented.

The story had been handed down through
the intervening generations as a mere family
legend, and with little idea that it would ever
be anything more ; but the late viscount had
treated it seriously, and had thoroughly imbued
Sir John Overton with the belief that he was
entitled, by the terms of the deed thus
executed between the old lord and Sir Robert,
to inherit the Hawkesbury estates. Sir John
had been even more astonished than disgusted,
when, on looking over the bundles of deeds
which Lord Hawkesbury bequeathed to him in
his will (with the remark that they contained
the proof of his title), this all-important deed
was not discovered among them. The late
lord had been far from methodical in his
habits. The huge deed-chest had not been
opened for years, and its contents were in a

state of utter confusion. After the most careful search, it became but too evident that the
deed was not there.

The new lord—who had spent his youth in
attendance at Carlton House, his middle age
in lounging at the clubs, and both in waiting
for his cousin's coronet—treated the whole
story as the hallucination, if it were not the
deliberate invention, of a vindictive old man,
who had threatened a thousand times to ruin
the heir whom he could not repudiate. He
had, moreover, made some sarcastic allusions
to Sir John which the latter had never for-
given ; and had shown an insolent triumph
which might have irritated a calmer tempera-
ment than the baronet's.

It was, of course, easy to guess the part of
the story which Mr. Vincent kept back. He
had had the good fortune to discover the missing deed. Lina had told Charlotte something
about a box with a false bottom, which Mr.
Vincent had found out, and underneath which
had been concealed the "will," as Lina called

it, but which was, no doubt, this very deed, which was all that was wanting.

As Adelaide listened to all this, and thought of Horace, and tried to persuade herself that her own presence was not the cause of Mr. Paston's high spirits, she felt as though life were almost too full, and there were almost too many people to care for, and too many things to think about. She herself was deeply interested in the fortunes of every one of the persons in the room, each of whom was in his and her turn deeply interested in many other persons who were not in the room, and so on—until it seemed to Adelaide as though she held some of the threads of an enormous web, which enclosed half the world in its meshes. Even her own interests were not wholly confined to the little company in which she sat. All through the evening, she had slipped her hand every now and then into the little bag which hung at her side, and which Charlotte had given her for a Christmas present. There was a letter from Miss Simpson in the bag. It had come on Christmas Eve, and it helped to make that Christmas so strange.

Miss Simpson, after seeming so much better last summer, had been slowly growing weaker all the winter, and now wrote to beg Adelaide and her mother to come to Bath, and see her once more. She had shrunk from asking them to take so long a journey in the winter, but when she heard that they were at Dockhampton she could not refrain any longer. Her brother was sadly troubled, she added, and for his sake, more than for her own, she entreated her dear young friend to come to her when she left Dockhampton.

On reading this, Adelaide had yearned to go that moment and minister to the dear lady who had no woman of her own blood to smooth her pillow, and stand by her dying bed. She took the letter to her mother, much fearing that she would refuse to go to a house of sickness and mourning. But to her surprise, Mrs. Firebrace said instantly—

" Of course we shall go. There seems to be

no immediate hurry; we can stay our full
time here.   My nerves are too sensitive for me
to dare offer to help in the nursing, but I can
attend to the poor doctor's comfort, which will
be a great relief to poor dear Miss Simpson, I
know.   It will be a very good time for Bath,
too.   And, of course, if anything did happen
while we were there, I could stay with Mrs.
Hanway, I've no doubt, till after the funeral."

"Oh, mamma, pray don't talk so!" said
Adelaide, almost in tears at this blunt allusion
to the all too probable end.

"Nonsense, Addy!   One must be prepared
for contingencies.   She says herself she's dying,
and every one could see she was all along.   I
was never deceived by that rally last summer.
That's the way with consumptive patients.   Of
course, it's all very sad, poor thing! though, to
be sure, she always had a crooked back, and
couldn't have expected to live as long as she
has.   But it will do you no harm for it to be
known she sent for you when she was dying.
I should not wonder if Horace were struck by

it. I shall take care to tell him the whole story."

Sophia discreetly kept the story to herself until after Boxing Day; and then, much to her chagrin, found that Horace knew it already from Mr. Paston, who had learned it from Charlotte, and who was a great deal more struck by it than Sophia thought at all desirable. She could only hope that he would talk of the circumstance with Horace, and thus, perhaps, do her work for her, after all.

With so many distracting thoughts, it is no wonder that Adelaide felt confused and a little weary, or that she shed some tears which no one saw, while Horace and Mr. Paston played a violin duet later in the evening, as a sort of *finale*. The music was very sweet and soothing, and it rested Adelaide, though it drew the tears from her eyes. It seemed easier to reconcile the conflicting duties, and the strangely mingled pains and pleasures of life, as she listened to Horace's plaintive cadences, and Mr. Paston's spirited melody.

The duet was at an end, and Mrs. Firebrace was saying that it was really getting shockingly late; when Horace, suddenly exclaiming, "I had almost forgotten the most important thing of all, Dick!" left the room for a moment, and returning almost immediately with a folded slip of paper in his hand, gave it to Vincent, saying, "There, my dear Dick, I am glad to place this in your hands before so many witnesses!"

"What is this?" asked Mr. Vincent, in evident surprise.

"It is a power of attorney to enable you to act for me. I told you I would not leave you in the false position with regard to Lambton and Rench which you so justly complained of. I have withdrawn all my business from their hands, and intend never to have any more to do with them as long as I live."

"Horace, this proof of your confidence almost overcomes me," said Vincent, who was extremely pale, and who seemed as though he could scarcely speak. "I could have wished you had selected some one else. But I will do my best."

"I'll risk that," said Horace, shaking him by the hand, and almost as much moved as himself. "I can hardly forgive myself for having exposed you to so much unpleasantness. But that is over, and you need never, I hope, hear Rench's name again."

"That is scarcely possible," said Vincent with a smile—Sophia said afterwards that he squinted horridly—emotion usually increased the slight obliquity of vision of which she made so much—"I am pretty sure to hear Rench's name a good many times yet, for his firm are Lord Hawkesbury's solicitors."

CHAPTER VI.

Under Prompter. Sir, the carpenter says it is impossible you can go to the park scene yet.—*The Critic.*

PRINCESS PARIBANOU (Miss Annesley), Prince Almansor (Mr. Culpepper), and the Magician of the Enchanted Garden (Mr. A'Deane), covered themselves with laurels on Boxing Night. There had been a moment when Mr. Kiddle's heart stood still, and Mrs. Kiddle (waiting at the wings to come on, in the character of the wicked fairy Sarcamanda) felt that now she could forgive Mr. Culpepper for his treatment of herself. The Prince Almansor, gallantly arrayed in a silvery doublet, in which he resembled an elegant walking cascade, stood wand in hand, and smote upon the Enchanted Rocks. But, alas for the uncertainty of human arrangements! the rock would not act. Thrice did Almansor make the fairy wand resound upon its enchanted surface, and thrice did the Magician's spell-bound defences hold out, unshaken (as they ought to have been, to their very foundations) by the counter-spell thus brought to bear upon them. At the third blow, the wand (gift of a beneficent family fairy) snapped in twain. The Prince stamped with rage, and glared furiously at the wings. The audience, who took this to be all a part of the play, listened in breathless silence, in the midst of which a voice was heard to say, in a hoarse but perfectly audible whisper—

" 'It where you see the crack ! "

Almansor did so—he was near-sighted, and was compelled to stoop at an unknightly angle before he could see it, having unluckily left his eye-glass in his dressing-room ; but the stubborn rock yielded at last, and with a hollow boom, disclosed a yawning cavern, far

down whose vaulted depths might be perceived the sunny pleasaunces of the Enchanted
Palace. The jeers of the audience, who by
this time understood the situation, were
speedily turned into shouts of applause, when,
with a tremendous clash and clang, rocks and
caverns fell away, and the Prince found himself standing in the very heart of the Garden
of Delight, surrounded by palms of the most
pronounced varieties, and roses by groves-
full; while a fountain murmured gently in
a marble basin, on whose margin birds of
extraordinarily brilliant plumage sat preening
themselves, all unheeding the presence of
Almansor.

From this point all went well. At the
close of the performance there was a universal
call for the manager. As he bowed his ac-
knowledgments, Adelaide thought him, even in
his plain evening dress, a more heroic figure
than any one else in the stateliest of Spanish
costumes. The delighted audience proceeded
to call for every one, beginning with Mr. Cul-

pepper, and ending with the stage carpenter, whom a sharp-eyed urchin at the extreme limit of the slips had identified as the owner of the mysterious voice, which had revealed to Almansor the secret of the Enchanted Rock. It was the same sharp-eyed urchin who first called for the carpenter, and who, on that worthy's appearance, greeted him with a shrill cry of "'It where you see the crack!" which was taken up in all parts of the house, amidst laughter and cheers.

All this was eminently satisfactory. Horace graciously shook hands with Mr. Kiddle in the green-room, remarking as he did so—

"You see, Mr. Kiddle, the *Louis-Quinze* costumes did not ruin the piece."

Mr. Warrener gave them a whole column in the *Post*, and spoke of Mr. Culpepper in such very pretty terms, that that gentleman declared he freely forgave the injustice he had done his *Horatio*.

"I'll tell you what it is, Larking," he said, after carefully perusing the editor's remarks for the fourth time, "I do best in a leading part. I don't mind if I tell you—in confidence, you know—that I don't find so full a scope for the bent of my genius, when I've got to play up to another man. I can always do better when another man's got to play up to me. Deuced odd, but so it is. One can't help one's idiosyncrasies. And every one must own, Larking, that the manager does take the wind out of a fellow's sails in a manner that's really hardly fair—'pon my word, it's not."

Mr. A'Deane was not quite so well satisfied. The *Post* said that it was almost sorry for the favourable reception of that gentleman's part of the wicked Magician, as it much feared that he would be thereby confirmed in a mannerism which could not be too strongly deplored. Mr. A'Deane did not like this, and he was not mollified by some further remarks of the *Post* on his undoubted capability in a certain limited range of parts, if he would but correct these faults of manner.

Mr. Culpepper was rather jealous for Miss Annesley, whose grace and spirit were much commended, but who was not sufficiently exalted above Mrs. Kiddle and the other ladies. Still, on the whole, Mr. Culpepper repeated that he forgave Mr. Warrener, and even considered him a very tolerable dramatic critic, making due allowance for him as a provincial.

The great success of the Christmas piece was not a subject for unmixed rejoicing to the manager, who was, as Mr. Kiddle expressed it, "all agog to go back to the legitimate." He intended to return to "the legitimate" with *Damon and Pythias*, and he spent every spare moment in studying the part of *Pythias*, for which he had ordered severely splendid classical costumes, which for once struck Kiddle dumb with amazed admiration. When at length he did find breath to speak, he only said that if Mr. Lancaster went on at this rate, prices ought to be doubled, for it was worth all the money only to see the dresses.

Mr. Lancaster was by this time a welcome

guest in several houses in Dockhampton which no theatrical manager had ever entered before ; and sometimes, on off-nights, he held a reception, at which the ladies did the honours.   Mr. Paston made the most of his opportunities. He could not get rid of Sophia, but he could compel her to explore every court in Dockhampton, and to follow the windings of every narrow street and alley in the old town, in the search for traces of the city wall.   Charlotte and Adelaide enjoyed these antiquarian expeditions (it was Theodore who gave them that name) ; but Mrs. Firebrace's temper was sorely tried by the pitching, over which she was kept going at a good round trot, and even then she could not always prevent Mr. Paston from giving her the slip, and taking Addy down unforeseen turnings, to show her an old gateway, or "some such nonsense."

Horace insisted that Mrs. Firebrace and Adelaide should stay to see *Damon and Pythias;* and Mr. Kiddle insisted that the Fairy Spectacle should run at least a month.

As Miss Simpson wrote that she was a little better, and seemed rather glad than otherwise of the delay, Adelaide consented; and if the thought of her dying friend often mingled strangely with the busy excitement of the life around her, it was impossible to be otherwise than satisfied when Horace was near, and when she could see that every day the shadow which had fallen upon him grew lighter.

But there were times when for a few moments Adelaide felt her heart wrung by a dreadful pang, the real cause of which she had never dared to ask herself. These were the times when Mr. Paston most plainly showed himself her lover, and not merely her friend, as she had tried to believe him. At such times, Adelaide thought of Miss Simpson with something almost like envy. After all, one need not, perhaps, pity her so much—she was going where there is no more pain. But the next moment, Adelaide would be ashamed of having let a little heart-ache make her forget how much she had to make her happy. And she was happy—very happy. Only of course she could not stay at Dockhampton always.

So January wore away, and the Christmas piece was to be taken off, and *Damon and Pythias* to be put on. And Adelaide would see Horace act, which Charlotte and she both agreed was the greatest pleasure to be enjoyed here below.

CHAPTER VII.

Queen Margaret. Seems he a dove? His feathers are but borrow'd.

It must not be supposed that Horace's rupture with his solicitors made no more impression upon the little knot of people to whom he announced it, than it probably has done upon those persons who may chance to read this narrative. On the contrary, Mrs. Firebrace had only waited till the ladies were safe back at their lodgings, to exclaim—

"What infatuation, to be sure! For heaven's sake, Charlotte, use your influence with your brother, and get him to reconsider this mad step! I never saw such infatuation!"

"I am very sorry he has done it," said Charlotte. "But I don't like to interfere."

"If some one does not interfere, Mr. Vincent will be the ruin of your brother. I am as certain of it, as that I stand here."

"Mr. Vincent is much less likely to ruin Horace, than Horace is to ruin himself," said Charlotte, rather uneasy at these foreboding words, yet feeling them to be wholly unfounded. "In business matters, Horace is just the man to be taken in by anybody. He never can distrust any one."

"He distrusts Mr. Rench."

"Mr. Vincent made him. Horace would never have thought there was anything wrong. I am sorry it has happened. Dear papa put confidence in Mr. Rench, I know, and I am very sorry Horace has left him; but it is a comfort to know that Mr. Vincent is such a clever man, and able to see through any one who tries to impose upon Horace."

"I declare, Charlotte, you are almost as infatuated as your brother. I half believe you like him, after all!"

"You quite mistake me," said Charlotte,

with a red spot on each cheek. "I can wish to be just to a gentleman who saved my brother's life, without wishing to marry him."

"You dear impulsive girl!" exclaimed Sophia, kissing her. "You are almost as generous and unsuspecting as your brother! But I am quite an old woman, you know, old enough to be your mother" (Sophia looked especially juvenile at the moment); "and it is my duty to warn you."

"Have you ever said anything to Horace about what you think of Mr. Vincent?" asked Charlotte, appeased in an instant.

"Good Lord, child! Do you thing I'm such a fool? He would tell Vincent, and Vincent would persuade him I was I don't know what! But *you* could give him a hint—he'd take it from you. And even Vincent would hardly dare set him against his own sister."

"But what can I say? I would rather Horace had kept with Mr. Rench, but I have nothing to say against Mr. Vincent. Indeed, I couldn't say anything, after—after what has happened."

"What nonsense, Charlotte! Because a man asked you to marry him—no doubt, for your money—for I won't give him credit for caring for you," added Sophia, hastily, as she saw Charlotte wince, "are you never to think any ill of him? Really, Charlotte, you carry generosity too far!"

"It is not that—altogether," said Charlotte, blushing and stammering. "There is Amelia —I could not bear him to think——"

"I never saw such Quixotic people!" cried Sophia. "Well, you must take your own way, and, of course, I love you all the better for it. But, for heaven's sake, never drop a word to Horace about what *I've* said. If you do say anything, let it come from yourself. You'll only do mischief if you mention me. Promise me, Charlotte dear, that you won't?"

Charlotte promised; but when she and Adelaide were alone, she asked her cousin (who had taken no share in this conversation) what she really thought of it all, and of Mr. Vincent.

"I do not know," said Adelaide. "It seems dreadful to suspect him of anything wrong, and mamma does take prejudices against people sometimes, and then she can see no good in them. And yet," Adelaide said this slowly and thoughtfully, and as if she did not quite know how to express her meaning, "I have sometimes wondered why I did not like Mr. Vincent better. I do like him, that is, I think he is very clever, and I am sure he would do anything for Horace. But I don't like him so much as I ought to, considering how good he is, and all that he does for Horace."

CHAPTER VIII.

Benedick.   Love me ! why, it must be requited.

As the time for their departure drew near, Mrs. Firebrace devoted much thought as to the best means of bringing Horace to the point. He had always been kind, and even affectionate, to Adelaide, but his manner towards her was too much the same as his manner towards Charlotte—Sophia could have wished him less kind and more lover-like.   It really did seem as though the idea of falling in love with Addy had never yet occurred to him ; and if this was the case, it was a thousand pities that some one should not put it into his head.   *That* Miss Overton was married, and Sophia was quite certain Adelaide had no other rival, and almost equally certain that Horace would instantly fall in love with Addy, if only some judicious person knew how to drop a hint at the right moment. And what moment so right as the present, when he must have begun to get over Lady Fidelle's abominable conduct, and had not as yet become interested in any one else? Sophia resolved not to leave Dockhampton without an attempt to discover Horace's feeling for her daughter. Mr. Paston furnished her with a very good excuse; she would confide her anxieties to Horace, and see how he took it.

Fortune favoured her beyond her utmost hopes. It so happened that Horace, calling one morning and finding Sophia alone, thought this a good opportunity to sound her on the very subject upon which she intended to sound him. So when Sophia observed with a sigh that this delightful visit was drawing to a close, he replied—

"You will leave some behind you, Sophia,

who will regret you quite as much as you can regret us."

"You are very kind to say so; but men are sad, fickle creatures," said Sophia, with a shake of her curls, and a plaintive tone in her voice, which was quite as good as a tear.

"There is a subject I should much like to know your opinion on, Sophia," said Horace, with more hesitation than was usual in him. "But I feel some delicacy in approaching it."

"You need have no delicacy with *me!*" cried Sophia. "I hope you feel more confidence in me by this time."

"Believe me, Sophia, I feel entire confidence in you. But what I had to say concerns Adelaide, and I feel some delicacy——"

"Am I not her mother? Can you hesitate at telling me anything which concerns my only child?"

"Nay, do not agitate yourself, Sophia," said Horace—for Mrs. Firebrace was all in a flutter. "I have nothing to tell. I rather wished to ask something."

"Pray speak plainly," exclaimed Sophia. "Consider a mother's feelings—do not keep me in suspense."

"It is simply this," said Horace, who found it uncommonly difficult to say simply what it was. "I have for some time observed—that is, I cannot but believe—perhaps, I should say, I have fancied——"

"What? You torture me!" cried Sophia.

"Have you observed Mr. Paston's admiration for Adelaide?" said Horace, thus driven into a corner.

Sophia did not answer for some minutes. She was only considering what it would be best to say; but Horace thought that she was overcome by her maternal feelings.

"I know it is always a shock to a mother to find that she no longer holds the first place in her child's heart," he began. But Sophia interrupted him indignantly—

"And do you think me such a selfish mother as that?" she said. "No! It is the dearest wish of my heart to see my dear, dear

Addy happy——" Here she broke off into a deep sigh.

" Am I to understand that you do not think Mr. Paston likely to make her happy? I assure you I have the highest regard for him."

" He is a most excellent young man," said Sophia, who now saw her road straight before her. "But we cannot command our affections——"

" Does Adelaide find it impossible to accept his suit?"

" My dear cousin," said Sophia, rising as she spoke, "this is a painful subject—*how* painful, you cannot know. Spare me, and ask me nothing."

Horace, who had also risen, stood wondering and irresolute. Sophia had moved towards the window, to conceal her emotion.

" I must ask," he said, as Sophia gave a smothered sob—" is Mr. Paston the cause of any unhappiness?"

" No," said Sophia, with another sob.

" Is any one else?"

Sophia did not answer.

" My dear Sophia, you must know that Adelaide is very dear to me—as dear as a sister. Pardon my claiming a brother's right—— "

" I may be mistaken," said Sophia, wiping her eyes and sighing. " But a mother's eyes are seldom deceived."

" I will not affect to misunderstand you, Sophia," said Horace, speaking in a lower tone. " You suspect that Adelaide has formed an attachment ? "

" Do not press me. Addy would hate me for ever if she dreamed I had betrayed her secret. Poor child, poor child ! I do not think you would ever despise her—— "

" Despise her, Sophia ! Good heavens, do you take me for a monster ? "

" I think you are the noblest and most generous of men, or I would have bitten my tongue off before I said what I have," said Sophia, turning her eyes on him for a moment and then looking away again.

"I suppose you have your suspicions as to who the person is?" asked Horace, in a very low voice, leaning a little over the table, and with averted face.

Sophia was silent.

"May I ask who the person is? Believe me, it is not curiosity which prompts the question."

"Cannot you guess? There is but one person it could be."

There was a long silence. Horace's hand still rested on the table. Sophia stole a glance at him now and then, and resolved not to be the first to speak. And Charlotte and Addy might come home at any moment! Sophia. felt that she must go into hysterics, if Horace was silent much longer.

"Sophia," he said at last, still in the same low voice. "I have loved. I shall never love again. I cannot offer Adelaide a heart so worn and bruised as mine. She deserves a far more passionate love than I have to give. I should wrong her—— "

" She is the best judge of that," cried Sophia cheerfully. " As for never loving again, that is all nonsense. You will love some one worthy of you, who will return your affection. And you will forget this conversation—or only just remember it enough to give Mr. Paston a hint that it is of no use." Here Sophia sighed once more, and added, " You insisted on knowing ; but I have done very wrong. For Addy's sake forget all that has passed. I shall never refer to it again."

Sophia left the room before Horace could reply. He was still there when the girls came in from their walk ; but he only waited to exchange the usual greetings—with a marked deference in his bearing when he spoke to Adelaide, of which she little guessed the cause.

" What beautiful manners Horace has ! " said Charlotte, when he had gone. " I am sure there is no one like him in all the world."

CHAPTER IX.

Some must watch, while some must sleep;
So runs the world away.

IT was the last day of January, and places had been taken in the Bath coach for Mrs. Firebrace and Adelaide.

Damon and Pythias had superseded the *Princess Paribanou*, and Horace had " made a hit" in *Pythias*. Mr. Culpepper was very respectable in *Damon;* but his figure was of the slimmest, and as he himself remarked to Mr. A'Deane showed to greater advantage in the romantic than in the classical style. Pallium and tunic (the latter of the severest Dorian cut) hung on him somewhat too loosely, and to some extent justified the unkind epithet of "clothes-horse," applied to him from the

gallery by a shrill voice, believed by Mr. Culpepper to belong to the identical youth who
had called for the carpenter on Boxing Night.
But Horace's really fine figure appeared finer
than ever. He wore his *chlamys* with a grace
which made all the ladies envious. His slow
movements, absurd sometimes in *Hamlet*, were
appropriate here ; he took the stage with the
true classic stride, and with most imposing
effect. If anything, he was a little too imposing — perhaps he somewhat injured the
general impressiveness of the scene when he
towered so vastly above Mr. A'Deane (a tolerably fine man himself, but who did not understand the true use of the *cothurnus*), and was
altogether so majestic, that it seemed amazing
how *Dionysius* could venture to take such a
liberty with him as to condemn him to death.
Then, too, grand as he looked while embracing
Mr. Culpepper, it would perhaps have been
better if he had not folded him so very closely,
that he seemed almost to swallow him up—so
that *Damon* emerged, looking more like a

crumpled thread-paper than a noble gentleman of Syracuse.

But these were minor matters. Horace was magnificent in *Pythias*. The *Post* had a rapturous leader on the revival of the drama in Dockhampton, and could not find terms warm enough in which to praise everything— from Mr. Lancaster's majestic personal dignity, to the splendour of his sandals.

Theodore Paston had not spoken. Mrs. Firebrace attributed this to her own watchfulness; but Theodore was not a man to be kept in check by any of the petty obstacles which Adelaide's mother threw in his way. Adelaide herself was the cause of his silence. He had begun to fear that Horace was his unconscious rival; and he knew that if this were so his one chance was to wait. But every week as it went by left him less hopeful. That was by no means a happy New Year to Theodore Paston; and, though his violin kept as strict time as ever, Charlotte observed that his playing grew week by week less spirited and more mechanical. His wild sallies no longer made Horace smile in spite of himself ; and he hardly even cared to defend his favourite art theories. Until very lately, he had believed Horace to be so engrossed in his profession and his unrequited passion, as to be indifferent to all beside. That Blanche was married was, in Theodore's foreign experience, little or nothing to the point. Had Adelaide been married, he felt that it would have been sacrilege to lift his eyes to her ; but Blanche had no such sacredness for him, and he would not have been nearly so shocked as he ought to have been, had Horace confessed that he loved her still. But within a very few days of Adelaide's departure, he had noticed a change in Horace's manner towards her—it had always been courteous, but now it was deferential ; in a hundred little ways — almost imperceptible to an observer who had not worn love's magnifying-glasses—he contrived to give Adelaide the place of honour. But when the time came to say farewell, it was Theodore who could not tear himself away from the coach door, and who cried, as the horses began to strain and the wheels to turn, " Do not forget me till you come again ! " while Horace stood, with the snow-flakes falling on his uncovered head, looking gravely and almost sorrowfully after the departing travellers. Charlotte stood beside him, smiling and tearful. She was to remain with her brother until her cousins' return, and they were then to go up to London together.

As the coach rattled out of Dockhampton, Adelaide felt as though she were passing out of one world and into another. Clocks and watches can mark mean time, but thought and emotion are the only indices of real time, and every man carries his own meridian about with him. Between Dockhampton and Bath, Adelaide went through a whole life-time of thought and feeling, while Sophia tranquilly dozed and read *The Elopement*.

Horace and Miss Simpson shared Adelaide's thoughts not very unequally. She would have almost died of shame if she had been told that she was in love with her cousin. There is however a considerable difference (for those who can distinguish between things that differ) between being in love and loving. Adelaide loved Horace as we love the saints and heroes—never dreaming of appropriating them. But her heart sank a good deal at the thought that this brief parting was but the prelude to other partings, and that she could not hope that life would all be like the last six weeks, or like those sad yet blessed months in London, after her uncle's death.

The thought of death seemed to press in on Adelaide from all sides. She very dimly remembered, or imagined that she remembered, her own father's death. Then the poor major had died, and then her uncle. And now, Miss Simpson was dying. Life was strong in Adelaide, and death seemed hateful. For a few moments, she felt as though she could not endure another week of darkened rooms and awful quiet; she blamed herself for having in thought blamed her mother's shrinking from a house with death in it. She looked very white and weary before they saw the lights of Bath, and the dim amphitheatre of hills—which seemed to Adelaide like walls that none might scale, shutting her in with death.

But when the coach stopped at the house in The Crescent, and Caleb Roffey, the doctor's servant (he had served Mr. Bolland before him), had opened the door, letting out a flood of cheerful light, and the doctor himself had come out to receive them, before their luggage could be discovered—much more, before it was unstrapped, and delivered over to them —these thoughts vanished, and Adelaide could hardly believe that death was near at all.

"You are exceedingly kind. I cannot express my sense of your goodness," the doctor was saying to her mother. He looked worn, and he stooped more. There was a troubled expression, too, on the long thin face, and a nervousness of manner—Adelaide felt that she hardly knew the doctor under this new aspect, and yet he was physically but very little changed.

Upstairs, in Miss Simpson's room, all her courage returned. Who could feel afraid of anything, with that pale face smiling on one ? Sarah Simpson had never been beautiful, except with the beauty of suffering, which had refined, and of resignation which had ennobled very ordinary features. But that night, as she lay following Adelaide with her eyes, her face was as the face of an angel. And Adelaide, sitting there silent after she had read aloud the psalms for the evening, wondered at her own dark and sorrowful mood, and thought that no earthly cares could ever again shut out the vision of eternal peace, which she saw shining so plainly to-night through Sarah Simpson's eyes.

CHAPTER X.

His life in low estate began,
And on a simple village green.

MRS. FIREBRACE made herself at home in The
Crescent with the best grace in the world.
She won Caleb's heart by the questions she
asked about Mr. Bolland, and the interest she
took in the doctor's early life.   She disarmed
the cook, who had been disposed to be dis-
tantly polite, by declining to order dinner.
She kept the doctor talking to her at des-
sert just long enough for him to feel how
deep was her sympathy, and at the same
time how fully alive she was to the importance of his studies, to which she was most
considerately anxious he should return, as soon

as he had allowed himself a proper interval of
rest. She visited the sick-room twice a day,
and was so sympathetic that she seemed to
stay almost twice as long as she actually
did, and to retire only because the intensity
of her feelings was too much for her strength.
Sarah Simpson thought her a weak, emotional
woman, of a clinging and dependent nature,
who probably leant on her daughter's firmer
character and stronger will, as though their
relationship had been reversed. In the scheme
Sarah had at heart, the harmless weakness of
Mrs. Firebrace's character seemed a circumstance by no means to be regretted—from
which it will be clearly seen that Sarah Simpson knew next to nothing of the world. She
had, in truth, had but little opportunity, and
her brother was in this respect not much
wiser than herself.

Dr. Simpson was the son of a village schoolmaster, in one of the midland counties. He
had very soon learnt all that his father could
teach him, and (the tradition ran) was one day

discovered weeping under a hedge, by the
clergyman of the parish, who with some difficulty elicited the cause of the boy's distress.
It seemed that the precocious urchin had
bought an old *Eton Grammar*, with pence
which he had earned at odd times. This pre-
cious fruit of his toil (which he produced, very
much the worse for age and wear, and with
the last page of the *Accidence* almost reduced
to a pulp by his tears) he had carried home
in triumph, and spread before his father's (as
he expected) delighted eyes. But, alas! the
worthy schoolmaster knew no Latin, nor
indeed any tongue but the vernacular, the
grammar of which he found sufficiently con-
fusing; and after poring over the already
well-thumbed pages for a whole evening he
laid down the book, with the disheartening
remark that *he* " could make neither head nor
tail of it, and had always heard that Latt'n
was a deal harder than English." With spirits
damped, but with resolution unabated, the boy
plodded his weary way alone through the

Accidence, making sad work with his quantities, and grievously perplexed by difficulties which a few words of explanation would have made easy. The defective verbs had very nearly driven him to despair, but he held out till he came to the first words of *Propria quæ Maribus*, and found himself cast suddenly adrift on a sea of Latin, with here and there a few words of unintelligible English. Even had he known (which he did not) that he would find these cabalistic sentences done into dark and doubtful English in the remoter abysses of the book, the knowledge would have helped him little. The English grammar, as expounded to the first class by his father, shed but a dim light on the Three Concords, and none at all on the Genders of Nouns. His courage failed at last—it seemed that all his labour was thrown away. " I thought I knew most o' this quite perfect," he said dolefully, as he concluded his brief confession ; " but very like I've learned it all wrong."

The clergyman was much interested. He

was an eccentric old bachelor of good family, and considerable fortune, and he could look back upon a not inglorious University career, which he had somehow never followed up in later life as had been expected of him. He had vegetated in his country rectory for a good many years; but his old scholastic instincts were instantly awakened by this village lad, who was crying because he could not learn Latin. He examined Nathaniel, and found that the boy had actually committed to memory the greater portion of the *Accidence*. But his scholarly ears were tortured horribly long before the rustic student had exhausted his Latin.

"Stop, stop!" he cried, as Nathaniel murdered Prosody afresh at each word he uttered. "You have not yet acquired the very rudiments of Prosody. This will never do! We must begin *de novo*, entirely *de novo*."

Nathaniel afterwards discovered this to mean that Mr. Bolland was going to teach him Latin himself; but he now stood before the parson

very disconsolately, while the latter muttered,
" Astonishing ! Extraordinary ! " and finally
exclaiming, " I'll see your father on Monday,"
walked off with the grammar in his hand.

Mr. Bolland not only allowed Nathaniel to
come to him twice a week for instruction for
some years, but interested himself so vigor-
ously on his behalf as in due time to get him
a servitorship. Young Simpson distinguished
himself greatly in classics, took holy orders,
and became a Fellow of his college. He had
but just been appointed one of the classical
masters of a Foundation School, when Mr. Bolland died, leaving everything he possessed to
his sometime pupil—probably the only one of
his parishioners in whom he had ever taken a
personal interest; and Nathaniel Simpson saw
himself at liberty to devote his life to the work
which had been his dream ever since he served
the commoners in the hall of Balliol. This
work was the preparation of a *Hebrew Grammar*, which was, he fondly hoped, to make the
knowledge of the Sacred Language more general.

He intended to call it, *The Hebrew Grammar Popularly Explained;* and under this title he had in the course of twenty years, issued two or three sections of a work which the learned declared to be on so profound and exhaustive a plan that it would be a *Thesauros,* to which deeply read Hebraists might refer their difficulties, rather than a " popular " exposition of first principles. To this labour of love, Nathaniel Simpson brought his prodigious patience and his vast memory. He believed that a wider general knowledge of the sacred tongue would tend more than anything else to the glory of God and the good of man, and he toiled with endless pains to fulfil his gigantic task.

In the affairs of this world, Dr. Simpson was almost ludicrously ignorant. It had cost him superhuman efforts to learn enough mathematics for his degree, and he was commonly believed not to know the multiplication table. But whether the doctor was at fault here or no, he never forgot to go and see his father

four times a year, and to leave behind him a
piece of paper, on which the multiplication
table came into play for the schoolmaster's
benefit. The old man lived to see his son a
Doctor of Divinity; he died shortly after Mr.
Bolland. Old Simpson's only other child was
a daughter, who had suffered many years from
spinal complaint. She did not share her
brother's extraordinary mental powers; but this
had not prevented a strong affection subsisting
between them. The doctor had on resigning
his mastership established himself at Oxford,
whither he removed Mr. Bolland's library—in
itself a valuable bequest; and here he lived for
many years with his sister, engrossed in his
great work.

He allowed himself no holidays; but
every day, for the space of one hour by
St. Mary's clock, he paced up and down
Magdalen Walk. In the worst of weather the
doctor might be seen, wrapped in a cloak of
great antiquity (tradition ascribed it to Mr.
Bolland), striding along, with bent head and

arms folded in his cloak. Lost in thought as he appeared, he was not wholly oblivious of the outward world, for he always returned the salutes of his acquaintance, though generally so long after they had passed him that it was a never-ending delight to mischievous under-grads to waylay the doctor, bow to him with the utmost respect, and watch his retreating figure, sure of beholding him uncover to the empty air before he reached the end of the walk. Many were the stories told of Dr. Simpson's harmless eccentricities and extra-ordinary absence of mind, and a good many of these stories were true. But whatever for-getfulness he showed in ordinary matters, he never forgot to visit his sister, in the room (the pleasantest in the house) which he had had fitted up for her. Hither, at certain ap-pointed hours, the doctor came, and talked to his sister of many things of which she under-stood little, but to which she gladly listened, believing it to be a comfort to Nathaniel to speak to some one, after being so long alone among his learned books. Here too the doctor, in his turn, listened meekly to Sarah's gentle reproaches on his neglect to have his hair cut— the only subject on which she troubled him. His other personal wants were attended to almost without his knowledge.

The tailor waited upon Miss Simpson, submitted his patterns to her, and took his orders. It was several years since the doctor had been so much as measured; and, thanks to his sister's accurate observation, the tailor generally contrived to produce a very tolerable fit— to be sure, the doctor's figure had changed very little in the last fifteen years. Nathaniel thankfully submitted to be thus provided for, in all but two particulars—he could not be persuaded to have his hair cut oftener than once a year (for which he was reported to allege Scriptural authority); and he would never wear any other cloak than that of antediluvian pattern, which he had found among his benefactor's effects.

About a year before Mr. Lancaster's death,

a change for the worse had become apparent in
Miss Simpson's health. The few friends who
had found her out in her sick-room were the
first to observe the change, and one of them,
the wife of the vicar of the parish, made an
opportunity to meet the doctor one afternoon,
and give him a hint that his sister was more
ailing than usual. It was no easy matter to
stop the doctor, when he was once started on
his constitutional; but Mrs. Graham was a
determined woman—she seized him by the
famous cloak, and held him fast. When he
understood her errand, he thanked her with
much earnestness, and then (quite forgetting
to wish her a good afternoon) went straight
home—to the alarm of his servant, who would
have been almost as much surprised to see the
clock of St. Mary's itself walk in, as to behold
his master half an hour before his time.

Sarah had already secretly consulted a physician, who had recommended her to try the
Bath waters; but she took an unfavourable
view of her own case, and was unwilling to

disturb the doctor, as she believed, to no avail. But his alarm once excited, he became almost practical. He called on the physician, and learned from him that the symptoms were those of incipient consumption, and that the best chance lay in the air and the waters of Bath. To the astonishment of most people, the doctor announced his intention of removing to Bath ; and there he had established himself, books and all, in the fall of the year preceding Mr. Lancaster's death. He even went a little into society, at Sarah's entreaty.

"You will be so lonely when I am gone," she would sometimes say to him. "I could not die in peace, and leave you in a strange place with no friends to comfort you."

The doctor always looked very troubled when Sarah spoke thus, and would gently take her hand, and ask in a beseeching voice, if she did not think she was deriving benefit from the waters. But he yielded, and would now and then spend an evening at some one of the many houses to which he was invited. It was

thus that he first saw Adelaide. Absent-
minded recluse as he was, he had been struck
by her unlikeness to the young ladies of Bath,
and had spoken of her to his sister. It was so
very rare a circumstance for Nathaniel to com-
ment on the persons he had seen, that Sarah's
interest was aroused, and she had made in-
quiries about Miss Grant, which resulted, as
has been already said, in a mutual acquaintance offering to bring the young lady to call
upon her.

It had been a great grief to Sarah Simpson
to think of her brother left alone in a world
where he was so little likely to make new
friends; and gradually the hope grew up in
her heart that in Adelaide—young, indeed,
but older than her years, she saw a wife for
Nathaniel. She was a few years her brother's
senior, and she scarcely realized that he had
ceased to be a young man. She saw no young
men with whom to compare him, and Nathaniel's outward appearance had undergone
no very marked change, to eyes which had

watched him day by day. Her natural delicacy kept Sarah from dropping a hint to
Adelaide of the hope which she cherished as
her only earthly wish; but she talked of the
doctor's goodness, of his talents, and his learn-
ing, until Adelaide looked up to him with the
veneration which she would have felt for a
father. She expressed her affection by all
those little attentions which come with so
lovely a grace from a daughter; and the
doctor accepted them with grave and tender
surprise, and pondered over them sometimes,
as he turned the leaves of the books of which
Caleb implicitly believed no one else in Bath
could read a single word.

Adelaide best liked to hear Miss Simpson's stories of the doctor's boyhood; of the
worthy schoolmaster, and the simple village
gossips, and the homely village life, and Mr.
Bolland's goodness and oddities. The famous
Eton Grammar played a great part in these
stories, and when, one day, the doctor happened
to come in while Sarah was telling Adelaide

all about it (for the ever-so-manyth time), she said—when he had gravely inquired how they both did, and had sat down in the chair which always stood ready for him—

"Nathaniel, I have been telling dear Miss Grant about the *Latin Grammar* that you saved up your pennies for. I should like her to see it, if you could find it without too much trouble."

"It is scarcely a book to interest a young lady, my dear Sarah; but if you wish to show it to her, I will get it," said the doctor, with a mixture of embarrassment and pleasure, and he gravely left the room. "This book is interesting to me and to my sister," he said when he came back (he was not long gone); "but to any one else it is of course of very trifling value. I remember I paid one shilling and fourpence for it, at the book-stall at Tamworth."

Adelaide took the book and opened it reverently. It was covered with coarse whiteybrown paper, which had probably been first used to wrap up articles purchased in the village shop. A good many of the pages were loose, but it was not dog's-eared.

"It has been well used," said the doctor, looking down on it as it lay on Adelaide's knee, and slowly pressing the outstretched fingers of one hand against those of the other.

"He saw it at Tamworth—seven miles off our village," said Sarah, "and he was so afraid it would be gone before he could earn the money to buy it."

"I was greatly afraid," said the doctor, still fitting his finger-tips together. "Did my dear sister tell you, Miss Grant, that she found out what I was doing, when I had almost earned the required sum, and gave me the last penny out of her own slender store?"

"Pennies were rather scarce with us in those days," said Sarah, with a smile full of the most unselfish pride. "I had been very ill all the winter, and the school had been broken up by the small-pox."

It was with exquisite delight that Sarah saw

a tear fall upon the limp discoloured page at which Adelaide was looking.

"Thank you for letting me see it," she said softly, as she gave the book back to the doctor.

CHAPTER XI.

Dear beauteous Death, the jewel of the just,
  Shining nowhere but in the dark,
What mysteries do lie beyond thy dust,
  Could man outlook that mark!
                    HENRY VAUGHAN.

THERE could scarcely have been a greater contrast than that between the life at Dockhampton and the life at Bath, so far as Adelaide was concerned. At Dockhampton there had been a constant succession of more or less exciting events, and more or less welcome visitors; while at Bath a very few morning calls, church on Sundays, and a couple of letters from Charlotte, were all which marked the flight of the days. Mrs. Firebrace had, of course, many more friends in Bath than her daughter, who had been at school or at Bath Easton during the years when girls usually make most of their friend-ships ; and these friends Sophia by no means neglected.

Charlotte seemed to be enjoying herself, to judge from her letters. She wrote a long account of Horace's doings, and had copied out for Adelaide a " masonic poem," which he had written (and recited, in the character of Shake-speare) to celebrate the visit of a grand-master. It seemed from a notice in the *Post*, which she also enclosed, that " Brother Lancaster " had won much glory on this occasion. Char-lotte added that Mr. Vincent was coming down again in about a fortnight, " to see Horace on business "—a phrase which highly incensed Mrs. Firebrace, to whom Adelaide read her letter.

It was on the very day that this letter arrived that an alarming change took place in Miss Simpson. Until now, she herself and all around her had apprehended no very imme-diate danger ; but a sudden failure of strength, together with other unfavourable symptoms, warned even the doctor that the end might not be very far off. She again somewhat revived in a day or two; but the doctor who had hitherto refused to believe that her case was hopeless was now utterly prostrated by grief, and could with difficulty restrain himself from giving way even in her presence.

As soon as she could speak a little, Sarah sent for Adelaide, and asked her if she would not rather go to her mother—Mrs. Firebrace was just now spending a few days with Mrs. Hanway, who also lived in The Crescent. But Adelaide would not go away. Even if she had still felt the shrinking from death, which had for a time overpowered her, she could not have deserted her post. Miss Simpson was always easier when she was there. There was no lack of neighbourly offers; but there was no one beside Adelaide whom Sarah had learned to regard as a friend. Mrs. Firebrace was only too glad that dear Addy could be of any use, and assured the doctor, with her blue eyes swimming in tears, that she had known what sorrow was and——

Here Sophia, whose nerves had been a good deal upset, burst into a genuine fit of crying. The doctor, already half-bewildered, made one or two attempts to console her, but could get no further than " My dear madam."

It was no great wonder that Sarah Simpson did not see in Adelaide's youth an insuperable objection to her becoming Nathaniel's wife. Adelaide was so gentle, so thoughtful, so self-possessed, that Sarah almost forgot the disparity of years ; and it was Mrs. Firebrace, rather than her daughter, who seemed the flighty young girl. Adelaide's every movement soothed instead of jarring on the patient. The well-meaning but muddle-headed woman whom Adelaide found installed as nurse, was not long before she regularly asked her advice, and deferred to her opinion on all occasions.

" I doubt, miss, you've had a deal of experience in illness ? " she said a day or two after the visitors arrived ; and Miss Simpson asked the same question, as Adelaide sat one evening by her bedside.

"Not very much."

"Then how do you know so well what to do, my dear?"

"I think knowing that you like me to do things for you, makes me able to do them," said Adelaide, simply.

"Ah, my dear, you will never know what you have been to me. God will surely reward you, my dear, though I cannot."

"I do not want a reward, dear Miss Simpson. I only wish I could do more for you."

"My dear, I wish you would call me Sarah— I have often thought of asking you to do so— it seems more as though you belonged to me;" and Miss Simpson laid her thin, fever-dried hand on Adelaide's, and said again, "God will reward you, my dear; and you will, I trust and pray, live to be a blessing to others besides me."

It was on a stormy afternoon about this time, that Sarah said something to her brother, which she had for months had it in her mind to say to him; she had thought not to say it until the very last, that it might have the force of a dying request—but that was when she had expected to live till May.

It was growing dusk. The wind, which had been blowing in gusts all the morning, had fallen a little, but every now and then a sheet of rain drove against the windows. The lamp was not lighted, but the fire filled the room with a cheerful glow, in which every object could be clearly distinguished. Adelaide, who was to sit up part of the night, had gone to lie down, and the brother and sister were alone.

"I have been thinking so much, Nathaniel, of what will become of you when I am gone," said Sarah, when in answer to her question he told her that he had done next to nothing of late, and that his work was at a standstill. "I know how hard it is to speak of it, Nathaniel," she went on, after waiting in vain for him to speak. "But if you *could* try to think a little of the future——"

"Sarah, you break my heart!" exclaimed the doctor, in a hoarse, broken voice. But Sarah spoke again, as calmly as ever—

"Dear Nathaniel, I could die so happy if you would promise me something before I go."

"What is it, Sarah?"

"Dear Nathaniel," said Sarah, holding his hand fast, and calming him at once by her touch, "promise me that you will marry— some good, loving woman, who will be more to you than I ever could."

"No one could be that. No one but you has known me all my life. No one else knows how to talk to me about our father and mother, and the days when we were young." He seemed to utter these words involuntarily—as though they were wrung out of him by intensity of pain.

"Our dear Miss Grant is never tired of hearing it all, Nathaniel. I trust you and she will often talk of our old home, and of me, when I am gone."

The doctor did not speak.

" Do not grieve so, dear Nathaniel. I should be very willing to go, if I could think of you happy, with a good and loving wife to take care of you. Promise me, Nathaniel."

" I have never thought of marrying, Sarah. And I am too old."

" Only forty-nine, Nathaniel."

" I thought it was fifty, Sarah."

" Only forty-nine, dear Nathaniel. You are five years younger than I am. Forty-nine is no age at all, for a man."

" You understand these things better than I do, Sarah. So I am only forty-nine? Not that there is very much difference."

" There is a great deal of difference, dear Nathaniel. Promise me that you will marry before your next birthday. It is my dying request to you."

" It is a serious step to take—so, at least, I have always understood," said the doctor, rather uneasily. " And I really know so few ladies——"

" That is all the better, Nathaniel. You do

not want a fashionable lady. You must marry a loving, affectionate woman, who will take care of you, and look up to you, and see that you are not disturbed in your studies."

"Is there any lady you would wish to recommend, Sarah?"

"I leave that to your own heart, dear Nathaniel. Oh, you have taken such a load off me. I have prayed for this, ever since I began to be ill."

"I have never felt the lack of a wife, thanks to you, Sarah; but I have of late sometimes wished that it had pleased God I should be a father."

At that instant, Adelaide came in. Sarah looked at her brother, pressed his hand tenderly, and smiled. Nathaniel understood this to mean that Adelaide must not know what had been said. He went away presently; but he looked at Adelaide very often during dinner that evening, and thought how blest the man would be who could call her daughter. This thought had taken such possession of him, that

when she rose to return to Sarah (who had
sent to hasten her a little), he rose too, and
instead of opening the door for her as he often
did, took her hand, and saying, " My dear
child, I hope you know that you are as a
daughter to me," kissed her gravely on the
brow and turned away.

CHAPTER XII.

He that hath found some fledg'd bird's nest may know,
    At first sight, if the bird be flown;
But what fair field or grove he sings in now,
    That is to him unknown.
                          HENRY VAUGHAN.

MISS SIMPSON seemed so much stronger that evening, that Adelaide was surprised to hear why she had been sent for earlier than usual.

Most Christian people, by whatever narrower name they may call themselves, agree in desiring, before they depart this life, to pledge the friends they must leave behind awhile, in the cup of immortality. Controversy has raged furiously around the sacred symbols, each sect in turn has rigidly defined their significance, each sect in turn has mingled the leaven of earthly passion with the Unleavened

Bread which came down from heaven. But we best learn the true meaning of these, as of all things, in the great crises of life; and, whatever they may think, most Christian people who have drunk that fruit of the vine by a dying bed, feel much alike.

It had been arranged that Sarah should partake of this solemn Farewell Feast on the morrow; but as soon as Adelaide entered the room to-night she expressed a desire that there should be no delay. The doctor, feeling that he could not command himself sufficiently, had already requested the rector of the parish to officiate, and Caleb went through the wind and rain to beg him to come at once.

Mrs. Firebrace was unable to be present— she had taken a cold, and feared a return of the quinsy to which she was subject, and was besides (as she said in her note) too much overcome to be able to bear the emotion attendant on so painful an occasion.

The rector's wife came, however, and her kindly sympathy was a great support to them all, through the brief but trying service. Sarah alone did not shed a tear—not even when Dr. Simpson buried his head in the bedclothes and sobbed like a child.

"Now there is no more to do," she said, when the rector in an unsteady voice had pronounced the blessing. Then she spoke a few words to the servants, and to faithful old Caleb, who had wept with his master, and bade them all good night, and once more blessed and thanked Adelaide. And then, with her hand locked in Nathaniel's, she turned her head upon the pillow and seemed to sleep.

No one went to bed. Caleb crept upstairs every half-hour through the night, and Adelaide stole noiselessly to the door and whispered, "There is no change."

And yet there was a change. Even by the light of the carefully shaded lamp the watchers could see the other shadow deepening on the sleeping face. But she had scarcely stirred, and her breathing seemed easier than for many nights past.

So they watched till the turn of night. And as it drew near, and their own pulses beat lower, and the morning seemed very far off, suddenly Sarah opened her eyes.

" Nathaniel ! " she said.

And in the saying of the word her soul departed.

CHAPTER XIII.

Romeo. With Rosaline, my ghostly father? no;
I have forgot that name, and that name's woe.

IN the days which followed, a great deal of the
care and responsibility which others appeared
to be bearing fell in reality upon Adelaide.
It was she who ventured to go into the study,
and half-coax, half-force the doctor to take
food. And it was to her that he broke the
silence which had terrified the faithful Caleb.
She gently beguiled him into speaking of
Sarah, and she persuaded him to go back at
once to Oxford, and not stay on alone at Bath,
as his first impulse prompted him.

Mrs. Firebrace, whose threatened quinsy had
passed off, was profuse in sympathetic notes,

which the doctor made into a neat packet and kept in his desk, but which he apologized for answering only verbally through Adelaide. She called on the day after the funeral, and so judiciously combined sorrow for his bereavement with interest in his great work, that the doctor began to reflect very seriously on his sister's last request, and to think that Providence was very plainly pointing to the best way of keeping his promise.

The ladies saw him safe off for Oxford, and then themselves took the coach for Dockhampton. Mrs. Firebrace was so unusually silent on the journey, that Adelaide forced herself to talk, in order to cheer her mother's spirits---naturally enough depressed, thought the daughter, by all which had happened. Sophia was certainly "hipped;" but two very important questions were occupying her mind, involving nothing less than her own and Addy's future prospects — and perhaps her pre-occupation was not wholly due to pure grief.

Sophia observed Horace very narrowly as he met Adelaide for the first time after their return, but she found it impossible to draw any inference from his manner. It was exceedingly tender and respectful—but that was natural under the circumstances, and Sophia herself stood a good deal in awe of Addy.

But she was not left long in uncertainty. Their stay was to be brief—Mr. Vincent was obliged to go back to town, and Horace wished them to avail themselves of his escort.

On the evening of their return to Dockhampton, Horace and Mr. Vincent sat up late, as usual, talking about many things. Suddenly Horace said—

" When did you last see Lady Fidelle ? "

" Just before I came down here. She is more sarcastic than ever."

" Dick," said Horace, after a pause, " I think that wound is almost healed."

" I am heartily glad to hear it ! Who is the fair physician ? "

" Physician ? "

"Yes. A woman always cures the wound a woman made."

"Ah! Dick, I fear me the wound rankles still—not that she can ever be anything to me again ; but it rankles."

"Sir Saville would, I fancy, say the same, with more reason. His wit is no match for hers."

"Are they unhappy?" asked Horace, moodily staring into the fire. "Yet how could she be otherwise ?"

"You have not told me yet who your physician is," said Vincent, presently, looking at Horace with a smile on his lips, and the cast in his eye rather stronger than usual.

"She may refuse to undertake the case."

"Who is she ?"

"My cousin Adelaide," said Horace, looking round at Vincent to see how he took it.

"I am rejoiced to hear it," he exclaimed. "Her mother is the only possible objection— a meddling woman, but luckily a fool."

The next day, Horace asked Adelaide to come into a small room which he called his study, and where he kept such properties, books, and musical instruments as he did not care to leave at the theatre.

He made her sit down, but remained standing himself, and did not speak for some moments. It was however no uncommon circumstance for Horace to fall into a reverie. Even when he began to speak of Blanche, Adelaide did not guess what was coming, until he said—

"I have told you this, because I felt that I owed it to you to let you see how little I have to offer any woman. The heart's first freshness can never be restored. I have still a faithful affection and a deep regard to give; but you deserve more than this—you deserve to be enshrined in a virgin heart."

Adelaide sat without the power to speak or move. She could scarcely even breathe—all her powers of body and mind seemed to be suspended, as in those trance-like dreams

between sleeping and waking; but she knew
what he was saying, and what she must
reply.

"I will not ask for an answer now," continued Horace. "If you do not despise the
poor wearied heart I offer you——"

Adelaide could not speak, but she stretched
out her hands to him. She was more beautiful
than Blanche had ever even seemed, and how
infinitely tenderer than Blanche could ever be!
But his unrequited love was too interesting to
be cast utterly to the winds. He loved Adelaide, and her only, from that instant; but he
thought he should have a stronger hold on her
if he played for a time at least the melancholy lover.

But here he over-reached himself. When
Adelaide found voice to speak, it was to tell
him that it would be very wrong to take him
at his word.

"You are unhappy," she said—and no one
ever knew what it cost her to say this. "You
turn to me, because you are unhappy, not

because you really love me. You will meet some one some day, whom you do love."

"I love you, Adelaide!" cried Horace, driven out of his sentimentality by the fear of losing her. " I was mad to talk so; Blanche is less than nothing to me now! "

Sweet as these words were to Adelaide, she refused to pledge herself to him, until he was quite sure; and with all his pleading he could not make her promise to give him an answer now. " In three months," she said at length ; and from this he could not move her.

CHAPTER XIV.

Overlook this pedigree.
King Henry V.

HORACE saw his visitors depart with a countenance so sorrowful, that Mrs. Firebrace's
heart sank very low—he had, she knew, been
deeply impressed by the hint she had given
him, for he had been more melancholy ever
since. But when they had all taken their
places, and the final farewells were being said,
he pressed her hand, and whispered, " You
will see me in three months from to-day," so
very significantly, that, had the coach not
been full, Sophia would have "had it all out
with Addy" before the next stage. Second
thoughts however are best; and Sophia,
having ample time for hers, arrived at the

conclusion that with Addy's peculiar character it was wiser to say nothing.

But Sophia was not in the best of humours. She had played her last card with Horace, and she was by no means sure whether she had lost or won. And she had with some difficulty persuaded Charlotte to make her home for the present in Queen Anne Street (instead of moping herself to death in Russell Square, with her old governess as her chaperone), with the annoying result that Horace had insisted on Mr. Vincent using the house himself, as he said, "to keep it warm." This was very provoking—if Horace and Addy ever came together, it would be highly desirable that Mr. Vincent should not continue in power ; and yet there were so many social advantages to be gained by Charlotte's presence, that Sophia could not back out of her proposal.

Prominent among these advantages were, of course, the Overtons, who were such very intimate friends of dear Charlotte's. They were still in town (with the exception of Gerald) ; and

Captain Overton, who called with his sister Lina, seemed decidedly struck by Adelaide— Mrs. Firebrace felt sure it was on her account that he was so set upon their going to see *Richelieu*, just brought out at the Lyceum. Sophia felt that she could under certain circumstances submit with resignation to the disappointment of her hopes with regard to Horace. It was rather hard, to be sure, to find Mr. Vincent cropping up even here—Sir John seeming almost as much infatuated with him as Horace was.

It was evident that Mr. Vincent's position had changed very much for the better. He was on the most friendly and familiar footing with Sir John ; and Mr. Counsellor Bingham had been pleased to say that, for a young man, Mr. Vincent had really a remarkable good judgment, and an extraordinary clear head—very much so indeed.

Of course, the law-suit was the chief topic of conversation. Sir John had lost a great deal more money than he could afford over

the former suit—so much, that he had felt
the pinch ever since. And Lord Hawkesbury
had insulted him in open court, and never
lost an opportunity of cutting jokes at his
expense. So marked had been his insolence
that Sir John had more than once sworn he
would call him out, but had been induced
by his wife and daughters to listen to reason,
and "treat the scoundrel with silent contempt."

"Though, demmy," said Sir John to Vincent, "I prefer loud contempt, for my part,
and so I've told my lady."

But now the tables would be turned; Sir
John could not contain himself. He showed
to the full as indecent a triumph as Lord
Hawkesbury had done, and talked in such
an outrageous manner, that Vincent and Mr.
Bingham had several anxious debates as to
the possibility of not calling him as a witness.

Lady Overton had so often declared that
she dared not be present in court—it would
be too much for her—that the ladies from

Queen Anne Street, who had long promised
to go, were a little surprised on arriving at
Westminster to see her waiting in the Hall,
with Lina and Amelia, while Sir John, Mr.
Bingham, Mr. Vincent, and the solicitors were
giving and exchanging last instructions. Mr.
Bingham's head, in his close counsellor's wig
with the black patch on the top, and Sir
John's bald head (very red and shiny indeed
this morning), went bobbing up and down
like a couple of floats when a big fish bites;
and Mr. Vincent (whom none of the ladies
had ever seen before in his wig and gown)
shook his little tails every now and then,
till Charlotte almost expected to see a sting
dart out. He was slightly flushed, and looked
very handsome—the grey wig suiting his com-
plexion as admirably as the gown did his
well-built though rather slight figure.

"Say as little as possible, and for God's
sake keep your temper," the ladies heard
Mr. Bingham say, as the little group seemed
to be breaking up.

"Trust me for that! I'll keep as cool as a cowcumber, demmy!" cried Sir John, so loud, that a rather coarse-faced gentleman who was passing at the moment heard him and turned round. Sir John started on seeing him, grew exceedingly red, and opened and shut his mouth with ludicrous quickness without however finding articulate speech. The gentleman took off his hat, disclosing a slightly bald forehead. He had a military appearance and was not very unlike Sir John, but many years younger.

"We shall be better acquainted before the day is out, gentlemen," said the stranger, making a sweeping bow. "Ladies, your devoted servant!" and with another bow he passed on.

"Bless me, he looks ten years older!" said Bingham. "He knows we can prove our case this time. Keep your temper, Sir John, for Heaven's sake—he'll lose his—I can see it in his eye. We *can't* lose our case, if only you keep your temper."

"Oh, demmy, I'll keep it. Only put me where I can't see that insolent scoundrel. He's a disgrace to the peerage, and so I'll tell him before I've done with him!" exclaimed Sir John, ramming his hat on his head. "Remember, Bingham, my right ear's my best ear, and don't shout too loud at me."

"We are sure to win, Sir John," said Vincent in his clear voice.

Charlotte did not know Mr. Vincent this morning. He seemed positively enthusiastic, and he actually jested as he escorted Amelia into court.

The court seemed quite full already, but Mr. Bingham and Mr. Vincent and several other gentlemen in wigs and gowns soon found places for the ladies. Charlotte's heart jumped into her mouth as she saw Rench, sitting by Lord Hawkesbury (the same gentleman who had passed them outside), and handing little notes along to the defendant's counsel, who whispered together, and looked about them, and seemed rather fidgety, till the jury had

taken their seats, after which they looked sur-
prisingly unconcerned.

The ladies themselves began to feel somewhat unconcerned before Mr. Bingham concluded his speech. The longer he spoke, the
less they understood what it was all about.
Adelaide thought that the jury yawned a good
deal; as for the judge, she could only see the
black patch on the top of his wig, and the
wriggle of the feather of his pen. Adelaide
thought he was taking notes, until Amelia
horrified her by whispering that he was probably writing letters—a piece of legal information imparted to her by Mr. Vincent. Once
or twice the judge lifted up his head, looked
under his eyebrows and over his papers at
Mr. Bingham, and asked a question, to which
Mr. Bingham always replied with a rustle of
his gown which reminded Adelaide of the
buzzing of a blue-bottle's wings—or, perhaps, a
wasp's, when he is just going to settle on a
peach. The resemblance was heightened by
a trick the judge had, while listening to the

answer, of switching his nose with his pen, as if he were brushing away some obtrusive insect.

While Mr. Bingham buzzed at the judge and droned at the jury (while only a few even of the lawyers seemed to be paying the least attention to what he said), Adelaide and Charlotte amused themselves by watching Mr. Rench, rapidly turning over enormous pages of enormous books—very much, Adelaide thought, as the upholsterer at Bath had turned over the leaves of his pattern-book, when her mother last repapered the drawing-room of The Cottage. Mr. Rench's finger ran along the lines as if he were pursuing an escaping sentence ; he always caught it however and instantly handed the book to his counsel, who would point it out to each other, and nod. Lord Hawkesbury once or twice wrote a note, screwed it up savagely, and passed it to his counsel, who seemed rather bothered. But Adelaide's eyes always came back from Rench's shrewd and eager face, and from Lord Hawkesbury's flushed and angry one, to Mr. Vincent. He sat perfectly still—only now and then jotting down a word or two on the sheet of paper which he held in his hand. Sometimes the faintest shadow of a smile would flit across his lips, but otherwise he sat there looking as though his thoughts were far away—and perhaps they were.

All of a sudden, Mr. Bingham sat down— to rise again for an instant, and say in a hasty mumble, "M' lud—learned friend—now address you."

It was a very exciting moment for all the ladies (Amelia turned the colour of a peony) when Mr. Vincent rose, and with a toss of those stingful tails, and a rapid searching glance round the court, which seemed to light on each several face in turn, and which yet scarcely made him pause perceptibly, began (the cast in his eye was very observable), " M' lud, gentlemen of the jury—— "

CHAPTER XV.

How much more elder art thou than thy looks !
Merchant of Venice.

THE moment Mr. Vincent began to speak,
every one in court became attentive. The
rustling and shuffling which had gone on while
Mr. Bingham slowly ground out his sentences,
and in which the words, "M' learned brethren
on the other side," and "M' learned friend who
is with me," came over a good many times,
ceased instantly. Before Mr. Vincent had
been speaking five minutes, the counsel on the
other side were listening with the deepest
attention, only now and then jotting down a
word or two on the margin of their briefs;
and the judge had laid aside his pen, and,

with his head leaning on his open hand, was following every word Mr. Vincent was saying.

It was very easy to follow him. He put the case before the court in a nutshell. In sentences which did not contain one unnecessary word, he showed the old Lord Hawkesbury, of George the Second's time, who doted on his only child, and was sorely grieved that his coronet could not descend to her son, at whose birth it was that he made the proposal to his heir-presumptive which resulted in the much-disputed deed of settlement. This same heir, too—a younger man than Lord Hawkesbury, but with sons of his own already, had the almost certainty of himself, and the probability of his children, succeeding to the Hawkesbury peerage, to set against the remote contingency of a failure of heirs-male in the unforeseen future. It was, Mr. Vincent urged, by far the wiser course for Colonel Mayne-Travers to take. Lord Hawkesbury was not yet fifty; and the birth of a son by a second marriage would have at once reduced the colonel's chances in the

future to almost *nil*, and have greatly embarrassed him in the present—he being deeply
involved. Mr. Vincent passed lightly over
the intervening generations, who had come to
look on this compact of their grandfather's as
a dead letter, never likely to take effect. But,
all of a sudden, continued Mr. Vincent, the
aspect of affairs was changed. The late lord
was a married man, but childless. He was
also a somewhat eccentric man—Mr. Vincent
would even go so far as to call him a very
eccentric man. He had very strict and un-
fashionable ideas on the duties incumbent on
persons whom it was the fashion to call "privi-
leged ; " he believed that a nobleman was
bound to be more and not less honourable,
more and not less honest, more and not less
truthful, more and not less just, than other
men. He had in vain striven to imbue the
mind of his heir-presumptive—the defendant
in this action—with these eccentric notions ; he
had even strong reason to believe that that
gentleman had in more than one instance

shown but a lax respect for the laws which
govern men of honour. Such at least was
Lord Hawkesbury's undoubted and undoubting
belief—whether right or wrong, it was not for
Mr. Vincent to say.

At this point in the counsel's speech, two
gentlemen in the back seats looked at each
other. Lord Hawkesbury's reputation at the
clubs was none of the best, and they did not
know how far a counsel was allowed to go in
raking up old stories. But Mr. Vincent,
having said so much in a manner which
plainly implied that he could say a great deal
more, went on to speak of the plaintiff, whom
he described as a man after the late lord's own
heart—a simple downright English gentleman,
who had discharged the duties of his station
with unostentatious fidelity. Here followed
a neat allusion to Peterloo, and to the unhappy disturbances taking place at this very
time at Manchester, and even in parts of our
island which we might well have hoped were
saved, by their very remoteness, from the perils

of anarchy. Was it any wonder, asked Mr. Vincent, if Lord Hawkesbury bethought himself, under these circumstances, of the tradition which his branch of the family had also preserved? He was wrong, indeed, to call it a tradition, since it was but very little older than the memory of many living men—the deed of settlement having been executed in the year 1758. Lord Hawkesbury had seen the deed—of which each of the parties it must be presumed originally had a copy, though that in the possession of Sir Robert Overton's father-in-law had never been found. Lord Hawkesbury had, Mr. Vincent repeated, seen this deed hundreds of times, had carefully docketed and preserved it, and had placed it for safety in an old family deed-chest, which, like many other articles of furniture made in a less civilized age than our own, had its secrets.

Here Mr. Vincent became slightly embarrassed, and went on with a little less confidence to describe how the missing deed had been discovered, unfortunately not before an action had been brought by the present plaintiff, which had, for want of this very deed, resulted in a nonsuit. It had occurred to the plaintiff (or to a friend of the plaintiff's—for on this point the learned counsel was not quite so clear as usual) to thoroughly examine the deed-chest itself, which had not hitherto been done; and the missing deed was discovered in a cunningly contrived receptacle, the position of which the jury would presently have full opportunity of examining for themselves. Mr. Vincent—perhaps because he was slightly nervous—had grown a little more vehement in his gestures, and had by a sudden movement of his arm disarranged the wig of Mr. Bingham, who happened unluckily to be in the act of rising to reach a law-book. There was a titter in court. Mr. Bingham set his wig straight, and the judge (who had not seemed to be looking that way) switched his nose and said something, at which there was another laugh. Mr. Vincent was, evidently put about by the little *contretemps*, and lost the thread of the sentence ; but he paused for a moment, scowled at the counsel on the other side, who had laughed more than any one, and recovering himself went on with greater fluency and clearness than ever.

Lord Hawkesbury's face was a very unpleasant study during Mr. Vincent's speech. When at its close Mr. Bingham stood up, and in answer to the judge's question, "Do you produce the deed-chest, Brother Bingham?" replied, with unusual briskness, "We do, m' lud," and clapped his hand on a large iron box, which rose from the heaps of papers and documents like a black rock from the surf—the defendant abruptly shifted the crossing of his legs, and gave a loud cough, or snort. Some persons in court said that he swore—at any rate, he took snuff copiously, and glared at Mr. Vincent, and then at Sir John, with bloodshot eyes which certainly did not convey blessings.

Adelaide and Charlotte used all their eyes and ears, but it was surprising to themselves to

find afterwards how very confused their recollections were. The jury examined the chest
with the utmost attention and curiosity. An
usher with a very evil countenance, who had
every now and then called out " Si-lence ! "
took it to them (they sat in two pews, as
though they had been at church), and seemed
to find it very heavy. Mr. Vincent stepped
over to them, and pointed out the secret spring
with his long, elegant fingers ; and the fore-
man himself drew the famous deed from its
hiding-place, and appeared much struck.

Lord Hawkesbury fumed, and was observed
whispering angrily to Rench, who only shook
his head. The chest was shown to the judge,
who made a joke or two, and then the deed
itself was minutely examined, and the signatures compared.

Sir John was put in the witness-box, and
got on pretty well, thanks to the ear-trumpet
which Mr. Bingham had insisted on his using.

A fierce-faced counsel on the other side next
made a speech, and was called to order by the

judge for abusing the plaintiff; "Especially as he cannot hear what you are saying of him, Brother Trowncepole," observed his lordship. There was a laugh at this, for Serjeant Trowncepole had a very peculiar, mouthing way of speaking, which it was difficult for even quick ears to follow.

The serjeant treated the plaintiff's claim with the utmost contempt. The condition, he said, was illegal.

"No condition is mentioned in the deed of settlement," interrupted Mr. Bingham. "There is a devise in tail-male to the heirs of the body of Evelina Overton, failing direct heirs in tail-male of the body of Augustus Frederick Mayne-Travers; but no condition is mentioned."

"M' learned friend says no condition is mentioned," observed the serjeant sarcastically; "but m' learned friend who is with him had a vast deal to say of the condition."

"We show the motive, and prove probability. Your side has asked why Augustus

Frederick Mayne-Travers should be a party to
a deed limiting the succession," said Mr. Bingham, ruffling his gown at the serjeant. " I
submit that we do not in any wise prejudice
our case in so doing."

Serjeant Trowncepole next urged that the
estates were what he called "a void remainder ;"
but here he became unintelligible to all but
lawyers.

The serjeant and the other counsel with him
having said their say, some gentlemen who
had studied handwritings were called to try
and prove that the signatures were not genuine.
All this, and a great deal more, was jumbled
up together in Adelaide's head in sad confusion. There was a good deal of examination
and cross-examination, which seemed to the
girls to have nothing to do with the matter in
hand. Perhaps the judge thought so too, for
at last he asked Serjeant Trowncepole whether
he had any more evidence to show that the
deed of settlement was not genuine.

" I have no more evidence on that point,

m' lud," said the serjeant a little flustered, and considerably out of temper with his client, who pestered him with continual notes.

" Then I shall direct the jury to find on that issue," said the judge. " It is the only material point."

Then judge and jury vanished, and a loud buzz of talking began. Lord Hawkesbury seemed to be having a violent quarrel with his counsel, who shrugged their shoulders till Adelaide thought their wigs would come off. And Mr. Vincent came and asked the ladies if they would take any refreshment, and Lady Overton and Mrs. Bingham went out with him ; but the girls all said they could not eat. Adelaide knew that Mr. Vincent was thrilling with anxiety and triumph, and knew also that triumph predominated, though he did not say a word to the ladies about how he thought the case would go. And then the court grew empty, and Adelaide noticed how dingy it was, and how the very air seemed dusty, and felt oppressive and suffocating, though the day was

very cold for April, and there had been a fall
of snow. And while she was wondering why
the place filled her with such gloomy thoughts,
Charlotte said, "Adelaide, I never knew a trial
was so horrid. I feel as though I were being
tried myself," and looked quite pale.

Then—Adelaide did not know how long
after—there was a little commotion somewhere
in the court, and the usher with the evil countenance cried, "Si-lence!" and there was a
rush; and in a moment the court was more
crowded than ever, and the jury had come
back; and presently the judge re-appeared
from the curtains behind the bench, and every
one was waiting in breathless silence, so that
there was no manner of need for the usher to
call (or rather to bellow) for "Si-lence!"
Then the names were called, and some one asked
the jury if they were agreed. Adelaide heard
only the word "Plaintiff," in the answer to
this question; but the next moment she saw
Sir John violently shaking Mr. Vincent by
both hands; and Lady Overton declared she

should faint, if Mr. Bingham (who was in the most extraordinary bustle, and seemed suddenly all shoulders) did not take her out into the air directly. And Amelia and Lina were laughing and crying together, while Mrs. Bingham, quite composed, said she had never had any anxiety, as Mr. Bingham always won his cases.

Just as the ladies were leaving the court, Adelaide remembered Lord Hawkesbury, and looked about for him. She could not see him anywhere; but Charlotte said he was still in court—she had caught sight of him standing over poor Mr. Rench, who seemed to be trying to slip away.

CHAPTER XVI.

2nd Gent. He will deserve more.
3rd Gent. Yes, without all doubt.

King Henry VIII.

IN the first wrath of defeat, Lord Hawkesbury had appealed ; but every one believed he would withdraw his appeal—as he ultimately did. But even before he did so, Sir John was in such a state of excitement at having gained a verdict, that Mr. Vincent seriously feared he would bring ·on a fit of apoplexy. Sir John celebrated his victory by a dinner, at which he drank the health of his counsel, and confusion to the Whigs—Lord Hawkesbury was a supporter of Lord Melbourne's Government.

"A pretty pass we're got to," he exclaimed, his face purple with patriotic ardour, and his

third glass of port—" a pretty pass we're got
to, with fellows marching about with swords
and guns under the magistrates' noses, and Joe
Hume wanting to improve the Reform Bill!
Pretty improvements he'd make, and a pretty
thing to improve!   Why, demmy, Vincent—
by-the-by, the only thing I know against you
is that your name's the same as that d—d
Radical of a Chartist—but that you can't help,
of course; can't change one's name every time
a d—d scamp happens to have the same.
And now here's O'Connell at it again, worse
than ever."

" O'Connor, Sir John, O'Connor—the physi-
cal force man—he made the row at Birmingham," shouted Mr. Bingham with unnecessary
vehemence in Sir John's ear.

" O'Connor, then, demmy—there's no difference between 'em that I can see—rogues
and traitors both.   I'd hang 'em both up, if I
had my way.   If the Dook was in, he'd soon
string 'em up.   Vincent, you shall go into the
House.   Bill or no Bill, no rascally Radical dare

show his nose in Cloppingford, and Copeland's getting shaky. When he pops off, you shall have his seat, my boy, demmy if you shan't!"

Sir John fell asleep soon after making this promise; and Mr. Vincent did not feel at all sure how far he might trust to it, especially as Mr. Bingham had looked rather glum when he heard it.

Mr. Vincent was most chivalrously attentive to Amelia, when the gentlemen joined the ladies. As he said to her, it seemed as though Fortune had turned her wheel, and as though his long train of ill luck had at last exhausted itself. "Who could tell," he said, almost playfully, "what might happen, or what good fortune might not yet be in store for him?" and then he checked himself, and said—with the gravest smile in the world—

"You see, Miss Amelia, how easily I could become presumptuous, and forget that I am only a poor, briefless barrister."

"You will have plenty of briefs now, Mr. Vincent; I heard Mr. Bingham say so to mamma," cried Amelia, who was growing quite at her ease with him. "And Annabella told me Mr. Bingham would be glad to serve you."

"Ah, Miss Amelia"—said Vincent.

Amelia blushed, and nervously smoothed out the ends of her sash.

Vincent took courage, and whispered (having first seen that Lady Overton was deep in conversation with Mrs. Bingham by the fire, and that the gentlemen were all talking together by the window), "Amelia, you know what I would say. Do you bid me hope? If fortune smiles on me, may I—— ?"

Here Mr. Bingham begged Mr. Vincent to step across the room, if he would be so good —sorry to interrupt a *tête-à-tête*—but Mr. Vincent's opinion was wanted on a disputed point.

Sir John had scarcely recovered his usual equanimity—which at the best of times could be only described as an "unstable equilibrium," when he was again thrown into a pucker by the resignation of the Melbourne Ministry. Great were the searchings of heart in South Audley Street. Lady Overton saw the Gatheringay coronet descending upon Sir Saville and Blanche, from a Tory heaven, where there were plenty of sinecures for younger sons. Sir John, who honestly believed that the Whigs were driving the country post-haste to ruin, and that Lord Brougham in particular was the latest incarnation of the devil, rejoiced less selfishly, but even more undisguisedly. As every one knows, these, and a thousand other like hopes, were destined to speedy disappointment. The Tories tried for too much, and lost all. The young Queen refused to dismiss her ladies, and surround herself with comparative strangers ; and foreign observers had a new instance of British incomprehensibility, when they saw Lord Melbourne and Mr. O'Connell defending the privileges of their Sovereign against the great Duke himself ; and heard Mr. O'Connell declare his solemn belief that, had the Queen yielded, she would quickly have been poisoned by the Tory ladies of the bedchamber.

The spectacle of the return of Lord Melbourne to power made Sir John more anxious than ever that Mr. Vincent should go into Parliament. He had frequently referred to the idea which he had mooted at the dinner he gave his lawyers ; and he now wrote to Lady Overton's brother, whose influence as chief landowner in the neighbourhood was very great at Cloppingford ; and, setting forth Mr. Vincent's merits, urged Mr. Lacey to use that influence in his favour, in the event of the seat becoming vacant. Mr. Copeland, a distant connection of the family, was in feeble health, and had, as Sir John knew, talked of accepting the Chiltern Hundreds.

Mr. Vincent's admirably lucid speech in *Overton* v. *Lord Hawkesbury* had already brought him several other briefs. When Horace came to town in June, he found the library table in Russell Square strewn with papers which did not relate to his own business ; and

Mrs. Staples informed him that Mr. Vincent often sat up half the night over his lawyer's work.

"Not down here, he don't," explained the housekeeper. "He works upstairs in his bedroom — I know he does, because Harriet says the candles is always burnt down to the sockets. *I* think it's very un'ealthy to work in your bedroom. P'r'aps, Mr. Horace, you could persuade him to set up in the library, if he must set up—but I wish he'd *get* up. Getting up's better than setting up, as I've heard say many a time."

Horace had but an impatient ear to lend his friend, who however insisted on having a long business conversation with him. In vain did Horace plead to be spared, and repeat over and over again that he could not be plagued with such paltry details, and that so long as he could carry on the theatre in a manner worthy of the legitimate drama, and pay his company punctually, he wished never to think about money or money matters—Mr. Vincent was determined, and after a little more remonstrance Horace sank back into his father's armchair, and resigned himself to Mr. Vincent, who thereupon laid before him a minute account of the state and prospects of British railways, and concluded by advising him to buy shares in the Leeds and Selby Railway.

"It is now in an unprosperous condition," continued Vincent; "but the York and North Midland are going to buy it, and, to my certain knowledge, the shares will be worth pretty nearly what the holders ask for them in a few years, and they will pay double almost immediately."

"Railways have been nearly at a standstill lately," said Horace doubtfully. "I don't care to lock up my money, perhaps for years, or else to sell my shares at a great loss."

"Railways will soon be another thing altogether from what they have been," said Vincent. "The directors have mostly been timid men, ready to lose all for fear of risking a little. Hudson is carrying on the York and

North Midland on a very different principle. In five years, if he lives, England will be a network of railways, and half the wealth and power of the country will be in the hands of railway directors. Now is the golden opportunity, before the rush comes ; in a year or two, every one with any money to invest will throng the market, and railway shares will be at a fabulous premium. You saw for yourself what the traffic already is on the London and Dockhampton line."

" I was astonished, I confess."

" Next year the line will be open the whole way, and the traffic will be a hundredfold. And in the north of England, on the lines which I should recommend you to invest in, the traffic will be a thousandfold."

" My dear Dick, I leave myself in your hands. I cannot pretend to be a man of business ; but as you put it, I perfectly understand the whole thing, and if you advise me to invest in the North Midland, I will authorize you to do so for me."

"I recommend the Leeds and Selby. But, with your wealth, there would be nothing easier than for you to become a director."

"Good heavens, Dick! You do not seriously propose to *me* to become a railway director? Why, Dick, I should play the part worse than poor Mrs. Kiddle played *Belvidera!*"

"Many directors do not attend the meetings."

"I would not suffer my name to appear under false pretences, Dick. A director who does not assist in the management, is only a shareholder, and he ought only to call himself such."

"At least, you need have no scruples about becoming a shareholder."

"Certainly not, if you think it safe. Now, if they would make you a director——"

"I must wait until I have made my fortune," said Vincent gaily.

"My dear Dick, why not allow me to invest a few shares in your name? Do not deny me. And if this seat in Parliament falls vacant, it will be necessary for you to shew that you have six hundred a year."

"Only three hundred, for a borough member."

"Well, Dick, if you undertake all this business for me, I shall insist on your accepting sóme shares. I'll say no more about it now ; I have more pressing matters to think of."

Of course when Horace said this Mr. Vincent could not detain him, even if he had wished, with any demurs. He hoped however to be making the three hundred a year needful for representing the borough of Cloppingford, long before that borough would require his services as its member. His prospects were improving there almost as much as they were everywhere else. He had met Mr. Copeland in South Audley Street, and had found him an elderly valetudinarian, fussily concerned for the welfare of his little borough, which he had represented for a good many years, and delighted with the interest Mr. Vincent took in railway extension. Mr. Copeland believed that he himself was an undeveloped engineer of a high order, and had made plans for most of the great engineering works executed during the last quarter of a century, each of which he was convinced was infinitely preferable to those of the engineers. He was particularly severe on Mr. Brunel; and nothing would do but Vincent must come to his chambers in George Street, and see *his* plans for a tunnel under the Thames.

Mr. Copeland had plans for everything; and among his projects was a branch line from Cloppingford, to join the North Midland, which Mr. Vincent promised to "look over at his leisure."

In the course of this interview Mr. Copeland perceived, though his young friend did not explicitly say so, that the said young friend knew a very great deal about shares and scrip, and had a very shrewd guess indeed as to which way the wind was going to blow across the money market, and in which direction railways were going to run, for the next ten years or so, to say the least of it. Sir John had told Mr. Copeland that his young friend was clever enough for a lord chancellor—here digressing, to express his opinion of " Broom ; " but Mr. Copeland was himself rather inclined to think that his young friend might prove another Hudson, and, if so, it was very much worth anybody's while to be civil to him.

CHAPTER XVII.

Lady Capulet. Marry, that marry is the **very**
    theme
I came to talk of. Tell me, daughter Juliet,
How stands your disposition to be married ?

IT would have been impossible to Adelaide to
have told her mother that Horace had asked
her to marry him. Sophia would have pooh-
poohed the delicacy which made her refuse to
give him his answer at once, and would have
been perpetually worrying her with the
worldly counsels and complaints which the
poor girl knew too well. It seemed to her
that she could not bear to marry Horace
when her mother talked about the advantages
of the match. This of course was folly ; but

Adelaide was not twenty, and had not yet learned to value worldly advantages.

Sophia on the other hand had long learned that Addy was peculiar; and this knowledge checked many a speech which she had a shrewd inkling might make her daughter only the more obstinate. But considerations of prudence are like umbrella-cases —we soon get tired of using them; and Sophia was less eloquent than usual on Addy's duty towards Horace Lancaster, chiefly because she had of late been speculating in another market. Adelaide had found it quite easy to be patient when her mother talked about Captain Overton—it is to be feared that she was rather glad than otherwise of his attentions (though she was much too honourable to encourage them), since they diverted her mother from a subject about which it was very hard to be patient. Sophia however had not forgotten Horace's promise to come to town in three months; and she always showed the keenest interest in the letters which Charlotte received from Dockhampton.

Horace had written pretty regularly, but had not been very communicative. He had spent the Easter holidays in writing something—believed by Charlotte and Adelaide to be a dramatic work, and spoken of by them with awe and reverence as "Horace's tragedy." Of course it was a tragedy. Horace would be sure to write a tragedy. He had brought out the *School for Scandal* since Easter, and had played *Charles Surface* with great success. Miss Greyson and Mr. Larking had left the company, and Miss Elton (whose voice Horace said was a decided acquisition) had joined it. The theatre was very well filled, and the only drawback was that the expenses were barely covered. Luckily, as Horace observed, money was not his object; and he had not lost any as yet, if he had made none.

Horace was to dine in Queen Anne Street, and Adelaide wore a white dress and yellow ribbons, which lighted up her rich colouring, and brought out a deep yet delicate glow, like the red of a damask rose, on her finely curved cheeks. Charlotte was still in half-mourning, but Mrs. Firebrace was resplendent in the lilac satin, over which she wore, to tone it down, a black gauze scarf.

Horace was looking well ; his manner was easier—he even laughed.

"I'm sure we're all charmed to see you looking so cheerful, with all your anxieties," said Sophia. "I shall never forget the turn it gave me, when I heard the Cheltenham Theatre was burned down. I thought of you directly, and so did the dear girls."

"You are very good," said Horace. "Kiddle has been lecturing us all about carelessness of fire, ever since."

"And quite right, too, Horace. I'm very glad he is so careful."

"My dear Charlotte, I am careful too—Mr. Paston is careless, if you like. Don't you remember how he stuck the candles all about the scenery, the night I took you behind ? Kiddle goes about after him with an extinguisher—at least Paston declares he does."

Adelaide's heart beat so fast, that she could hardly hear what the others said. Was it really true? Had Horace asked her to marry him? And were the three months gone, and was he here to demand an answer this very day? And would the others, who knew nothing about it, ever go away?

And then somehow, and as it seemed, all in a moment, dinner was over, and the ladies had retired to the drawing-room, and Horace came in; and Adelaide looked round and saw that they were alone. And by the time she had got over the fright and flurry of her spirits at finding herself face to face with him, they were sitting close together on the sofa, and Horace was holding her hand, and bringing forward one good reason after another for their being married in August.

Mrs. Firebrace was in her own room, reclining in a dimity-covered armchair, and reading a novel, when she heard a tap at

her door. She had but just time to hide
the book in the depths of the chair, before
Adelaide entering with most unwonted haste
threw herself into her arms, and burst into
tears.

"What on earth is the matter, Addy?"
cried Sophia. "Here, child, take a handkerchief—you're spoiling my satin!"

"Oh, mamma, I'm so happy!" sobbed Adelaide, accepting the handkerchief, but still
clinging to her mother.

"What! has Horace proposed to you?"

"Y-y-es, mamma—he did three months
ago."

"Then, why on earth are you crying now,
child?"

"I only said Yes, to-day, mamma."

"Good gracious, Addy! What on earth
made you hesitate a moment?"

"Be-because," sobbed Adelaide, "I wanted
him to be sure he didn't like B-Blanche
b-best."

"Nonsense, child! Blanche is married, and

it would be very wicked for Horace to like her now," said Sophia severely.

"Y-yes, I know it would," said Adelaide, "but I wasn't sure."

"Well, Addy, I'm very glad it has all turned out so well as it has. I was sure it would, from the first, if you only knew how to play your cards well. After all, he's a better match than Captain Overton, for everything except the title."

"Oh, mamma, how I wish you would understand that I don't care for a title! I would rather marry Horace than be Queen of England!"

"Then don't let him know it. It is always safer for a woman not to let a man see how fond she is of him—it keeps him faithful. I should never have kept the poor major in order if I had been like you. Men are all alike, and it doesn't do to let them think you're very fond of them—they take advantage of it. I've had more experience than you, Addy, and I can tell you that the best way to manage your husband is not to let him think you are wrapped up in him. That was always my plan with the major, and it succeeded admirably."

CHAPTER XVIII.

Lady Frugal. You say right :
There are counsels of more moment and importance,
On the making up of marriages, to be
Consider'd duly, than the portion or the jointures,
In which a mother's care must be exacted.

The City Madam.

HORACE'S reasons for hastening his marriage
were quite conclusive to Mrs. Firebrace, and
Adelaide's objections were very feeble.   He
could scarcely take a holiday of more than
a few days until next Easter; while if the
marriage took place in August he would have
a clear month, and could take Adelaide on a
Continental trip, which he had already planned
out in his own mind.   Sophia, who had spent
her first honeymoon in Paris, thought this
a most delightful idea.   Adelaide would have

been content to go anywhere with Horace ; but even for her, " the Continent " had a romantic charm, heightened by her early recollections of strange lands.

Long before the first of August came, Adelaide thought two months quite long enough to be engaged. Fortunately, there was no house to be furnished. Sophia made a vigorous attempt to " set up a proper establishment " for the young couple at Dockhampton, but Horace would not hear of it. He was, he said, merely serving his apprenticeship. He hoped before another year to leave Dockhampton for a wider sphere, and he refused absolutely to do anything which even looked like settling down there. He was almost angry when, in reply to something he had said about the expense of two complete establishments, Sophia suggested that he could let the house in Russell Square. Sophia lost her temper a little, and could not help saying that she had forgotten Mr. Vincent wanted the house.

" Sophia," said Horace gravely, " I have

more than once observed with pain that you
do Vincent injustice.   If you can forget that
he saved my life at the risk of his own, I
never can."

"You cannot expect me to like him as well
as I do you, my dear Horace," said Sophia,
who shewed she was hurt.   "But if I have my
own opinion of Mr. Vincent, I can keep it to
myself."

But if Adelaide was spared the toils of fur-
nishing under her mother's auspices, Sophia
kept her fully occupied with her *trousseau*.   It
was delightful at first to go shopping every
day, and buy beautiful silks and muslins and
laces, which Horace would see her wear.   But
even shopping palls upon one at last.   When
for the twentieth time we have sat down on
the long-legged and short-backed chairs which
an obsequious shopman has set for us with a
professional flourish, for the twentieth time
become aware of another obsequious shopman
(with a pliable spine) demanding what he can
have the pleasure of shewing us, and for the

twentieth time produced the list which we
drew up instead of enjoying our breakfast—
shopping becomes a bore.   And legitimate
shopping was but the half of Adelaide's toils.
When they reached home—Sophia as brisk as
ever, but Adelaide with a headache—there
would be the laceman waiting in the hall with
a pile of boxes containing goods on approval ;
the milliner sitting on a chair behind the
back parlour door, with three bandboxes on
the table ; and the dressmaker upstairs in
Mrs. Firebrace's dressing-room, with a dress
which had already been altered twice.   Every
room except the drawing-room was strewn
with half-made gowns—one waded through
yards of gauze and muslin ; the chairs were
hung with shawls which Sophia was not sure
she should keep—Sophia did no little shopping
on her own account—and bonnets, which she
must see Addy try on with the dresses they
were to be worn with.   Even Charlotte, who
had always dressed more elaborately than
Adelaide, confessed she was sick of the sight

of new clothes, and declared that the house smelt like a linen-draper's shop. Sophia was terribly indefatigable. If ever the girls slipped away for a little talk, they were sure to hear a knock at the door, and a voice informing Miss Adelaide that her ma' wanted her, please, as there was some gloves come for her to look at; or the shoemaker with the sandals; or the woman with the underlinen—and would she come down directly?

But two months cannot last for ever (though it does sometimes seem as though they could); and even the last fortnight, which was worse than all the rest put together, and the last week, which was worse still, came to an end. This last week, with all its racket, scamper, and confusion, was marked by one event, which as time went by grew more and more prominent in Adelaide's memory. Time is a more judicious artist than we know. In the bustle and hurry of the days we often confuse events together, as of equal importance; or perhaps some little matter of ordinary routine gone wrong distracts our attention from the unusual (but unostentatious) interruption, which we shall hereafter look back upon as *the* event of that day—nay, of many days and years.

Thus Adelaide, full of cares—by this time grown ordinary—about the fit of a gown, heard that Dr. Simpson was below in the drawing-room, with a mind pretty evenly divided between emotion at his visit, and a lively sense of the pervading confusion and discomfort, so remote from her visitor's habits and character. She hastily disengaged her head from the bonnet (which had already been the cause of much worry, and which had considerably disordered her hair), slipped into her morning-gown, and had almost reached the drawing-room door, when she heard her mother calling, "Addy! Addy!" in a loud whisper; and looking up saw Mrs. Firebrace's pretty yellow curls depending in a graceful bunch over the balustrade.

"Come here a minute, Addy," said Mrs.

Firebrace, still in a whisper. "Remember, though Mr. Hillyard is coming to the wedding, he has not yet been asked to give you away. I purposely only invited him to the wedding. Don't forget. I shall come down in about a quarter of an hour."

So saying, Mrs. Firebrace whisked herself lightly back again to the dressmaker; and Adelaide went down to the doctor, feeling rather more bewildered than before.

During the months which had elapsed since Miss Simpson's death, Mrs. Firebrace had taken care that Dr. Simpson should neither forget nor be forgotten. She wrote herself to inform him of Adelaide's engagement, and the doctor replied in a letter which Sophia declared showed more good sense than she had expected in such a bookworm. In spite of Adelaide's dissuasions, Mrs. Firebrace invited him to the wedding; and began instantly to debate with herself the possibility of his acting as father on the occasion, in the stead of Mr. Hillyard, whom Adelaide had had the bad taste to suggest.

"Though I don't suppose," she observed to Charlotte, "that he was ever at a wedding in his life, or would have the remotest notion of what he ought to do. But any one would be better than Hillyard."

The doctor, as Adelaide had anticipated, excused himself on the plea of his recent bereavement, "which rendered him unfit to take part in a festive occasion." This, Sophia protested, was "quite ridiculous," poor Miss Simpson having been dead very nearly six months.

Sophia was correct in supposing that the doctor would be at some loss how to comport himself at a wedding; but he resembled many other distinguished persons in not being so great a fool as he looked. He dimly remembered having heard of such things as wedding presents; and he astonished Mrs. Graham by calling upon her, and solemnly asking what she considered a suitable gift to a young lady who was about to be married. Mrs. Graham had not spoken to Dr. Simpson since, on a cloudy autumn afternoon now nearly three years ago, she had stopped him under the elms, to warn him of his sister's danger; and she confessed to her husband that her first thought was that the poor doctor had gone mad—so impossible did it seem that he should know a young lady who was going to be married! He perceived Mrs. Graham's surprise, and briefly explained who Adelaide was; whereupon the good lady put on her bonnet and marched him off to the nearest jeweller's, where, under her instructions he ordered a handsome bracelet, which he put into his breast-pocket as carefully as though it had been a portion of the manuscript of his grammar, only appearing a little surprised at the difference of shape.

Adelaide found the doctor sitting bolt upright in an armchair, in which he looked more than ever like a seventeenth-century theologian—of the period before divine right went out, and full-bottomed wigs came in.

"My dear young lady," he said, taking her

hand, and holding it with the utmost deliberation, "permit me to wish you every earthly blessing in the marriage state, into which your dear mother informs me you are about to enter. It is an institution which has received the Divine sanction—indeed, it is the most ancient of all institutions, as we learn from Holy Scripture, dating back, in fact, to the time of man's unfallen innocence. I trust, my dear young lady, that you may enjoy much comfort and profit in the marriage state. I have ventured to take the liberty " — here the doctor gravely relinquished Adelaide's hand, fumbled in his pockets, and became much less fluent in speech than before—" to offer you—ah, here it is—a slight token of my esteem and affection. I—I did not trust to my own judgment in the matter. I consulted a lady of much experience, and I trust that a judicious selection has been made."

" Dear Dr. Simpson, how kind of you to take so much trouble ! " said Adelaide, with the tears in her beautiful, wistful eyes.

"I assure you, my dear young lady, that I look on you as a daughter, and that any little trouble I may ever take on your behalf is the greatest possible pleasure. It is, indeed —though, in the present instance, the greater part of the trouble, as you are good enough to call it, was kindly undertaken by Mrs. Graham."

During this speech—delivered slowly, and with a certain hesitation, which would have been called "humming and hawing" in an M.P., but which somehow did not seem at all the same thing in the doctor—Adelaide opened the parcel, and Mrs. Firebrace entered the room. Even Adelaide, well-used as she was to her mother's company manners, was struck by the artless effusion with which she greeted the doctor.

"I shall feel terribly lonely when dear Addy is married; but I am rejoiced at her happiness," said Sophia, wiping one of her pretty eyes, and looking tenderly at her daughter.

"Surely, my dear madam, you will still be much together?"

"Ah, doctor, you are too good to know what cruel things the world says of poor mothers-in-law. And young married people are best left alone. I shall not be one of those exacting mothers who expect their daughters to pay them as much attention after they are married as they did before. We are none of us perfect, and I am a poor creature at the best," said Sophia, with a Spartan smile and a feminine tear; "but I am not so unreasonable as that. And so long as Addy is happily married, it does not much matter what becomes of *me*."

"Indeed, you distress me, my dear madam," said Dr. Simpson. "There must be many to whom your happiness is very dear."

"I shall be just the same, mamma," said Adelaide, who was not entirely blind to her mother's power of extracting enjoyment even in her daughter's absence.

"Of course you will, Addy dear, if I will

let you.   But your first duty will henceforth
be to our dear Horace."

"I believe the gentleman is your cousin—
a Fellow of Queen's, I think?" said the doctor.   "I must have frequently seen him.   I
believe, too, that he is at present devoting
himself to the drama?   Professor Rimster, of
Oriel, was talking about him the other day.
I remember he especially remarked the ac-
curacy which Mr. Lancaster displayed in
costume.   *Damon and Pythias* was the drama,
I remember.   By the way, Pythias is an error
—it should be Phintias."

"Our dear Horace has taken up acting
more as an amusement than anything else,"
said Sophia, jealous for her future son-in-law's
reputation.   "He was brought up to the
Bar."

"Nay, my dear madam, the drama is, or
has been, eminently influential.   And although
the less cultured Romans at one time regarded
actors with some contempt" (here the doctor's
courtesy all but got the better of his learn-

ing), "among the Greeks, tragedy was invested with much of the sacredness of religion ; and we are told that the Father of the Greek Tragedy acted his own characters. I was never in a modern theatre," added Dr. Simpson, as though he had personally assisted at the first production of the *Persians* and *Prometheus* and *Antigone;* "but I am aware that there are great and important—I may say, radical, differences between a Greek tragedy, and even a drama like this one of *Damon and Pythias.* Pythias, as I observed, is a misnomer. I was once present at Westminster School, when the scholars played Terence's *Heautontimorumenos,* and I remember being exceedingly interested."

It must not be imagined that the doctor delivered this speech in a breath. It was many times interrupted and a new direction given to the doctor's thoughts by ejaculatory remarks from Mrs. Firebrace. That experienced lady seeing the doctor thus set off on the subject of the Greek drama, considered it high

time to bring him back to more practical
subjects, and at length allowed her eyes to fall
on the bracelet, which Adelaide had some time
ago laid on the table for her to see.

"I'm sure it is a most handsome present!"
exclaimed Mrs. Firebrace. "And the newest
fashion, too! What charming taste you have,
my dear doctor!"

"I am very glad you approve it, my dear
madam," said Dr. Simpson, much gratified.
"But I must disclaim your compliment to
myself. I am indebted to a lady of great
judgment in these matters."

"My dear doctor, I am sure you yourself
have a most admirable judgment," said Sophia.
"There is no one I would so readily defer to."

"I assure you, my dear madam, I do not
deserve your good opinion. In fact, I feel
myself at a sad loss, since—since my dear——"

The doctor, who had been all along in a
very emotional mood, here broke down, and
pulling out a large white silk handkerchief
wept without disguise. Adelaide timidly

stroked his hand, and wished he were her father, that she might put her arms round his neck and comfort him.

The doctor adhered to his resolve not to make one of the wedding party; but he was in church on the wedding morning, in a retired pew where only Mrs. Firebrace espied him.

There is no need to describe the wedding, which took place by Horace's desire at new St. Pancras'. Mr. Vincent was his best man, and Charlotte chief bridesmaid—a rather awkward arrangement, but which could not well be avoided. And it would have been quite as awkward had she fallen to the share of Gerald, who had come home on leave, just in time to be asked to the wedding.

Mr. Hillyard gave the bride away. Adelaide had yielded so many points to her mother, that Mrs. Firebrace was both astonished and outraged when Addy expressed her wish that her uncle Hillyard should be asked to give her away, and that her cousins Sophy and Bessie should be two of her bridesmaids. Mrs.

Firebrace represented herself as astonished,
annoyed, hurt—but in vain; Adelaide was firm.
Uncle Hillyard, she said, was the only proper
person. He had been exceedingly kind to her,
and had helped Horace so much when he was
at Bristol.

"The only proper person, Addy!" interrupted Sophia. "Why, Sir John would be
quite pleased to be father. You are a great
favourite with him. I believe you might have
done even better than you are doing—but
perhaps it's as well as it is. Horace will be
easier to manage, and Charlotte will never give
you any trouble, as that stuck-up Lady Fidelle
might have done. But as for being the only
proper person, I must say, Addy, I'm astonished at you! Why, even Mr. Meadows
would be better than a drysalter!"

"I prefer my own relation, mamma," said
Adelaide, without a trace of temper, but also
without a sign of yielding.

"He's no relation by blood," said Sophia
sharply. "Poor Anna! she never was in the

least like me. But to think that a sister of mine could marry a drysalter—and he never even looked like a gentleman—and object to the poor major, who had mixed in the very best Indian society, and never had anything to do with trade in his life! I must say I think it very hard that a child of mine should do as you are doing, Addy. I'm sure it's not my fault. I'm sure you never saw *me* forget what was due to my position. But you always were obstinate. I'm sure I shall be thankful when you are married. I've been on thorns lest you should go and make a fool of yourself. I do believe you'd be proud of marrying a man without a penny!" Sophia had by this time talked herself into tearfulness. "And those vulgar girls!" she went on.

"You have not seen them, mamma, since they were babies."

"Do you taunt me, you unkind girl? You know perfectly well that your aunt treated me abominably when I married the poor major— poor dear man! how he did swear, to be sure, at Anna's letter!" This was perfectly true—Adelaide had heard him. "And as for seeing them, pray when did *you* see them, miss?"

"Horace says they are very nice girls, mamma. Pray do not be angry. I will give up having them, if you like; but I must have uncle Hillyard. And Horace wishes it."

"Horace is as great a fool as you are yourself!" exclaimed Sophia, whose language when she was angry sometimes recalled the poor major to Adelaide's memory. "But, there, have your own way!"

Sophia was going to add that she trusted her daughter might never repent her undutiful stubbornness, with some other remarks of the kind; but Amelia and Lina Overton were opportunely announced, and Adelaide escaped for that time, Mrs. Firebrace's thoughts being diverted from herself to Lady Fidelle, who it seemed was coming home, after her long honeymoon. There would be grand rejoicings at Sir Saville's country seat (Claverings—Lord Gatheringay's place), said the girls; and Mrs.

Firebrace felt that it would be a thousand
pities if Horace's ridiculous fancy for Lady
Fidelle (of which Sir Saville, too, knew nothing)
should prevent the Lancasters from receiving
an invitation sooner or later to visit Claverings.
As for the momentous question of providing
dear Addy with a suitable (though but temporary) father, Horace settled it himself. In
obedience to a hint from Charlotte, he wrote
that it would much gratify him to pay this
compliment to his cousin Hillyard, who had
deserved a great deal more of him than this,
in return for the exertions he had made on
his behalf on the occasion of his *début* at
Bristol. Sophia sighed—and yielded.

Mrs. Firebrace was a mistress of the royal
art of making a grace of necessity. If the
Hillyards must come, any undesirable impression which their manners and appearance
might create should be neutralized. Had
Mr. Hillyard been a classical scholar, he might
have been reminded of the cloud, *multo amictu,*
wherewith the goddess enwrapped those two

wandering Trojans whom she met in the wild wood, as dawn was breaking on the Libyan shore. In such a cloud (woven, in the modern instance, not of thin air, but of the finest manners) did Mrs. Firebrace envelope her brother-in-law and her nieces. So surely as any of the genteeler guests addressed a few words to Bessie, so surely did it happen that Mrs. Firebrace would float past at the instant, and gracefully cover the girl's plebeian confusion with some remark which turned the guest's attention from Bessie to herself. Sophy, who was inclined to be pert, and who called Mrs. Firebrace "aunt," before Sir John himself, as coolly as though her own father had been a baronet, caused poor Mrs. Firebrace the most lively anxieties as to what she would say next. But Mr. Hillyard was the worst—luckily, he was also the easiest to manage. He could not make Sophia out; it was incomprehensible to him that this was his wife's own sister.

"I remember she always had high notions,"

he said to Sophy; "but your poor mother kept her under a little. I'd like to see anybody keep her under now! Not that there's much harm in her little whims about being so mighty genteel; but I can't come up to 'em."

Mrs. Firebrace took care to sit between him and Sir John at the wedding breakfast, the more effectually to prevent the honest dry-salter from committing himself; and she more than once saved the family honour in the very nick of time.

"Now, Mr. Hillyard, you *are* so funny! You *do* say such odd things!" Sophia would say, playfully shaking her curls and her taper fore-finger at him. "I declare you're quite a character. *So* like my poor dear uncle! Ah, Sir John, it would have rejoiced his heart to see this day."

Thus did Sophia—with a smile in one eye, and a tear in the other—nip Mr. Hillyard's budding speeches. It was a little trying to have one's own brother-in-law blurting out, in the vicinity of a wealthy baronet with several peerages in his family circle, allusions to the " ware'us ;" and he really need not have observed quite so often, that " plain G. H., of Bristol city " would be happy to do anything in his power for his niece Adelaide or her husband—not, of course, dear reader, that you and I are not far above the weakness of wishing to suppress our drysalting connections.

Horace returned thanks for himself and Adelaide, in an eloquent but perhaps rather too elaborate speech ; and Mr. Vincent, for the bridesmaids, in a very elegant one, during the delivery of which Amelia blushed furiously. Even Captain Overton made a speech, but he shone less than Gerald, being considerably less self-possessed.

At last even the wedding breakfast came to an end, and the bride retired to prepare for her journey. She shed a good many tears, and kissed her mother a great many times, as she put on the handsome travelling dress, which Sophia trusted would be pronounced *distaingy*.

"I'm sure I hope you'll be happy, child," said Mrs. Firebrace, when Adelaide was nearly ready. "And now you're married, Addy, I do hope you'll use your influence over Horace, and make him take his affairs out of Vincent's hands. I don't suppose you could get him to break with Vincent altogether at first—you must watch your opportunity for that. You must begin by countermining him little by little."

"Dear mamma, why should I set myself against Horace's friend?" said Adelaide—too happy to resent these prudent counsels as she did at other times.

"Because you'll never get your own way with your husband, till you've got rid of Vincent."

"But I don't want my own way, mamma."

"Then what on earth have you married him for? I declare, Addy, I've no patience with you! Do you mean to be his slave?"

"Horace would never make any one his slave—much less me, mamma! You don't know him, or you could never say such a thing of him," said Adelaide a little indignant.

"Nonsense, child! Do you think I don't know what men are? If you don't begin at once with them, they'll get the upper hand. A wise woman finds out how to manage her husband before the honeymoon is over. You mark my words, Addy—if you don't keep Vincent in his place, you'll live to repent it. And any woman could manage Horace—he's not like the major, who required a great deal of tact sometimes, when he was in one of his obstinate fits. Though I'm sure you're quite as obstinate, Addy, and when it's too late you'll be sorry you didn't take your poor mother's advice."

And then they went downstairs; and amidst showers of tears and kisses and old shoes the bride and bridegroom got into the carriage and drove off. Adelaide looked out of the carriage window at the last moment, and saw Charlotte

throwing her own satin slipper, and her mother
(in her new gown of the most delicate imaginable shade of puce) waving a lace-edged handkerchief, while uncle Hillyard and Sir John
flourished silk bandanas. Behind these
crowded the other guests, but Adelaide only
saw their faces blended in an indistinguishable
mass, which reminded her for an instant of the
mass of faces she used to see in the Dockhampton Theatre.

It was Vincent who shut the carriage door.

"God bless you, Dick! I leave it all to
you," said Horace as he wrung his friend's
hand.

"Don't look back, Adelaide! Don't look
back!" cried Charlotte as the horses answered
to the coachman's whip and rein.

And as Adelaide drew in her head, she felt
Horace's arm clasping her close, and heard
him say—

"Now I can defy fate and fortune, with my
good genius at my side!"

CHAPTER XIX.

If she be not good to me,
What care I how good she be ?

IT may have been observed that Mr. Paston
was not present at Miss Grant's wedding.
This was not for want of an invitation—
written by Sophia, who, the moment Theodore
ceased to be dangerous as a lover, remembered
that as a connection of the Overtons he was
desirable as a wedding guest.   Young Lochinvar attended the bridal feast of his lost love
—but young Lochinvar did not expect to ride
away from Netherby Hall alone.   Theodore
was not a man to die of unrequited love—he
was too much of an enthusiast, and perhaps
also had too strong an interest in life, for the
sake of all that Theodore Paston might do in

it. But Adelaide was his ideal of womanhood; mentally, morally, and physically, she fulfilled his dream of the perfect woman, and he could not see her prefer another to himself without deep and abiding pain. He intended to live his passion down. The world held other women, faithful, tender, and charming — he was aware of one such, who had looked upon him not unkindly, and whose image had the power to console him even now. But Adelaide was his ideal—she was his *Adelaïda*, whose name was uttered by the evening breezes and the whispering may-bells, whose likeness he saw in Alpine snows, and in the clouds of declining day. To her he had dedicated (she did not know it) those still unpublished compositions which had awakened the echoes of Hampton Court, and whose melodies still haunted Charlotte's dreams. Theodore's dreams were haunted by visions of Adelaide's stately beauty moving among the somewhat undistinguished, but eminently aristocratic Court ladies of Vogelheimsburg, of the duke dancing the German waltz with her, on a ducal birthday; of operas, written and conducted by Theodore, to which Adelaide should listen with all her soul in her magnificent eyes. She was to have been the inspiration of his life, and all his laurels were to have been laid at her feet.

Of course, Theodore Paston had not lived in the land of elective affinities without becoming aware that another man's wife can be quite as eligible an inspiration as one's own; but Adelaide was not a woman of this sort, nor—to do him but bare justice—was Theodore much attracted by the romance of unlawful love. Even in its mildest, most harmless form of sentimental friendship, his pride revolted at a great deal which to the poetical manhood of Vogelheimsburg seemed so full of zest. Perhaps his English blood made him feel as he did; at any rate, young as he was, he was fully convinced that the position of a husband was far more dignified and secure than that of any *cavaliere servente* whatever. There was a stubborn something, very deep-rooted in his nature,

which made it impossible to him to worship
any other man's wife. At an age when most
English boys think girls were made expressly to
bore them, Theodore had already planned out
his future career ; and in this career a lovely
and adored wife was the central figure. The
moment he saw Adelaide, he installed her in
the place of this figure, which, he firmly
believed, had always worn her exact linea-
ments. She was *Adelaïda*—and *Adelaïda* was
lost to him ! His pain was sharp and endur-
ing ; he grew thin and pale, till Horace feared
he was ill, and stuck fresh daggers into the
poor musician's heart by the solicitude which
he displayed. When Sophia's letter came, in-
viting him to the wedding, Theodore locked
himself in his own room for an hour (to the
distraction of Mr. Kiddle, waiting with the
week's programme), and then went to Horace,
and, speaking with more hesitation than usual,
asked for three months' holiday, "to visit his
parents."

Theodore added that if he went to Germany

at the end of July, he could return at the
beginning of November, in ample time to
rehearse the Christmas piece. Horace, whose
perceptions were quick when he was not too
much absorbed in his own reflections to exercise them, glanced at Theodore's face, and
checking himself in the act of saying, "But
you will surely stay for my marriage?" sent
for Kiddle (by this time in a state of exaspera-
tion), and bade him advertise in the *Era* for
some one to temporarily take Mr. Paston's
place. After which, Horace was for some days
so sombre of mood, that Miss Annesley told
Miss Elton she believed Mr. Lancaster had had
a lover's quarrel with Miss Grant. Miss Elton
however was against this view, having once
seen Miss Grant, whom she described as a very
romantic-looking young lady, but far too gentle
to quarrel with her lover. Miss Elton added
that Mr. Lancaster was most likely unhappy
about poor Mr. Paston, who was going home
for his health. Miss Elton further informed
Miss Annesley—the two ladies were bosom

friends at this period—that she had always thought it would have been a match between Mr. Paston and Miss Grant; while as for Mr. Lancaster, she had fully expected to hear he was engaged to that handsome Miss Overton. From which it will be seen that Miss Elton had made a good use of her opportunities, and was an observant young person.

Miss Elton (who boarded with the Kiddles) was an enthusiastic admirer of the manager, whom she considered far more romantic a person than Mr. Culpepper. Mr. Kiddle's habit of speaking in private of the manager as though he were a troublesome ward, who would quickly come to ruin but for the interference of his guardian (Mr. Kiddle), excited much indignation in Miss Elton's breast. She considered Mr. Lancaster too good for these coarse and common surroundings; and she thought that Kiddle was trying to bring down the manager's lofty genius to his own low level, and despised him accordingly. Kiddle however thought a good deal of Horace. He

greatly admired his fine stage presence ; and
was not as averse as the editor of the *Post* to
his mannerisms and affectations. It was his
choice of plays, and not his mode of playing,
which drove poor Kiddle to say that Mr. Lancaster had no more idea than a child how to
catch the public. There is a poetical injustice
in life—which yet, in its deepest issues, is seen
at last to be justice—whereby our good deeds
are more heavily visited than our evil ones.
The Dockhampton public would have par-
doned (if indeed it did not rather admire)
Horace Lancaster's most glaring faults, if he
would but have been guided by Mr. Kiddle's
unerring judgment, and stooped to the illegitimate drama, with a liberal ballet. The
manager's lofty aims hindered his success ;
unhappily, they did not hinder his faults.
Many good, but morally rather feeble persons,
are sorely scandalized at Nature's—man's—or
God's (call it which you will—it is all three)
stern refusal to condone the means for the sake
of the end. To such persons there is a kind

of injustice in the fate which so often befalls good intentions. Our robuster forefathers could say without wincing that hell was paved with them; they saw deep into human nature, and knew what mere intentions are worth, and that they are often but a golden name for a tinsel ambition. He who would do good deeds must go deeper than intention; if he do not, he will be but one more in the list of self-deceiving egoists, who in all ages and nations have brought discredit on the noblest aspirations of man. He who would save the world, must know the world; Well-meaning must walk by the light of the lantern of Well-knowing. A wise man once said that nothing is so demoralizing as a sense of duty. To remember this would answer many a painful riddle. But it is not less true—nor, deeply enough considered, is it less compatible with eternal justice—that failure often comes, or seems to come, from what is best in a man, and not from what is worst. Misfortune will for ever seem more conspicuous than error.

CHAPTER XX.

Wellborn. I think I am in a good way.
Marrall. Good! sir; the best way,
The certain best way.
                    A New Way to Pay Old Debts.

IT is a popular delusion to suppose that the
vulgar mind is credulous. The vulgar mind
(in the modern sense of that adjective) is
eminently incredulous. Its first instinct is re-
jection, not acceptance, of everything presented
for its belief—save only that it can always
believe any fact which is sufficiently ugly.
The vulgar mind flatters itself that it is a
first-rate critic of art and literature, because
it is so firmly persuaded that the extraordinary is generally only the false, written
in five syllables instead of one. But here the

vulgar mind commits the same error which
they commit who deny miracles. The extraordinary is in reality more common than the
ordinary. One favourite dogma of the vulgar
catechism, in that section devoted to the arts,
is that coincidences happen more often in
books than in real life; the fact being that
authors are constantly compelled to water down
real life, in order to render its extraordinary
coincidences credible to the vulgar mind.
Life itself is too sensational, too dramatic,
too tragic, to be swallowed whole in those neat
pills which we call works of art.

One strange feature of life, vulgarly attributed to the invention of book-makers, is the
tendency of events to crowd together. Even
the vulgar mind sometimes quotes the proverb,
" Misfortunes never come alone." But events
never come alone. From murders downward,
events come in clusters. It is so in the life of
the world, and in the life of the individual.
Life never stands still—something is always
happening; but there are periods when we

seem (like happy nations) to have no history—
tracts of comparatively uneventful monotony,
separating us from epochs when one event trod
so fast on the heels of another that we had
scarce time to breathe, and no time to think
and understand what was happening to us.

The next few months were such a time of
calm to Horace and Adelaide. But the world
is like the sea—it may be high water at one
place, half-ebb at another, and low water at a
third.

Just when Horace was tasting as near an
approach to monotony as his character and
circumstances rendered possible, Mr. Vincent
began to find life eventful and stirring. A
whole morning spent in examining Mr. Copeland's plans had been followed by many other
interviews with that gentleman, all highly
satisfactory to both parties. Mr. Vincent instantly perceived the superiority of Mr. Copeland's plan for the Thames tunnel to that of
Mr. Brunel. He even pointed out a merit of
which Mr. Copeland himself had been hitherto

unaware. There were, besides, several dinners at the Carlton, at which Mr. Copeland's plans for the Cloppingford branch line were fully discussed together with many larger projects. The results of all this to Mr. Vincent were an invitation to Bleasbrook, and a perceptible widening of the circle of his acquaintance in London. It was generally believed that Mr. Vincent was in the confidence of the chairman of the York and North Midland Railway; and the knowing ones fully appreciated his discretion in not boasting of his intimacy.

"He'd be perfectly inundated by fellows wanting an introduction," said McLasher, a young barrister who had met Vincent at the Overtons'. "He's a sharp fellow, is Vincent, and he doesn't want all the shares to be bought up yet—he knows what they'll be worth in a year or two."

Mr. McLasher was known to have bought a few shares in the Leeds and Selby, at Vincent's advice; and a good many other persons were more or less directly influenced by Vincent's somewhat reluctantly given opinions. For Vincent never volunteered to talk on the subject, except to Sir John and Mr. Copeland, and to Horace Lancaster; but his reticence only increased the belief in the value of his opinion.

At Bleasbrook, the branch line was more seriously discussed. Mr. Copeland invited several of the neighbouring land-owners to his house, and exerted himself more than he had done for years, in the attempt to submit a feasible plan to Mr. Hudson, whom every one already knew to be the ruling spirit of all the North of England railways. Mr. Copeland underwent much vexation in the course of these efforts for the good of Cloppingford. One of his neighbours was averse to a railway at all, and to railways in general. Another was very willing to have a railway which should not pass through his own land. A third, whose land happened to be rather poor in quality, was willing to be compensated for a much larger portion than was likely to be required; and took dire offence at Mr. Vincent's remarking that the *détour* he proposed would be sheer waste of the company's money.

Mr. Vincent left Bleasbrook with reiterated promises of "running over" sometimes from Overton Manor; and Mr. Copeland constantly spoke of him as "a young man certain to rise to eminence." Sir John received him no less cordially, and with him, too, there was much talk that autumn on subjects highly uninteresting to the ladies.

"Bore's you, does it?" said Sir John, one day at dinner to Lady Overton. "Why, demmy, my lady, if half that Vincent says comes true, I shall be able to pull down the rickety old house, and rebuild it! Whim o' mine, all my life, Vincent, but never could afford it before. Too many bouncing girls to marry off, eh?"

Here Sir John winked at Vincent, who replied that a very few years would show that the most sanguine expectations fell short of the truth as to the future of railways.

Mr. Vincent said this as calmly as though he had thought that Sir John's wink referred solely to my lady's ignorance of her own interests, or some such harmless matter; but as he finished his glass of madeira (Mr. Vincent seldom drank port), he wondered rather uneasily whether Sir John suspected the state of affairs between himself and Amelia. Mr. Vincent had made the most of his opportunities with that young lady, and Amelia had assured him that she would be true. He walked about the gardens of Overton Manor with the ladies after dinner, while Sir John slept off the effects of a perhaps too generous repairing of nature; and there were many paths in the gardens too narrow for four persons to walk abreast. On these occasions, Lina would contrive to draw her mother on with her, and leave Amelia to follow with Vincent. But though Lina did this, she did not in her heart like Mr. Vincent, and she was very sorry

that Amelia did. She had even said so once
—provoked into unusual anger by an unkind
comparison which Amelia made between Mr.
Vincent and Horace—but had the next
moment implored forgiveness of her sister with
tears. Still, Lina did not like Mr. Vincent,
and she permitted herself the luxury of saying
so in her letters to Charlotte.

Lina received one letter from Adelaide. It
was written from Paris, and was full of delight
at the beauties of the Rhine. Paris, said
Adelaide, was splendid, too; and they had
been to the theatres, which were finer than
ours, though, in her opinion, the acting was
very bad—at least, in tragedy. In comedy, it
was very clever, no doubt, but there was
nothing so good as the *School for Scandal.*
She and Horace had had their portraits taken
by the new daguerrotype method. The like-
nesses were very good, if you looked at them
in the right light; but she would always
prefer miniatures on ivory. There was a good
deal about the sights of Paris which, said

Adelaide, Horace knew a great deal more about than any of the *Suisses*, or even than the guide-book itself. But delightful as it all was, she would not be sorry to come home; for after all you could never feel at home in Paris. She and Horace had been quite excited in reading the accounts of Captain Wade fighting his way through the Khyber Pass. Horace had said that he envied Captain Wade.

Lina read a good deal of this letter aloud, at the general request. When she came to the part about Captain Wade, Mr. Vincent said that any man would be willing to run a considerable risk with the chance of distinguishing himself.

"Of course!" cried Lina. "Think of the glory!"

"Doubtless Captain Wade thought also of the value of the glory," said Vincent. "Glory, Miss Lina, has a substantial, marketable value, to which sensible men never pretend to be indifferent."

Lina did not more than half understand

Mr. Vincent ; but she retired to read and re-read her letter in a distant part of the kitchen garden (which had been her favourite retreat as a child), more convinced than ever that she did not like him.

CHAPTER XXI.

Petruchio. Now, for my life, Hortensio fears his widow.

FOR some time past, Dr. Simpson had been much exercised in mind. He considered himself to be under some sort of obligation to marry, or at least to make an effort to marry, before he should attain his fiftieth birthday. He had not absolutely promised Sarah to do so, and had even intended to dissuade her from urging it on him, had not her death followed so quickly on the conversation in which she had exacted what, to the doctor's scrupulous conscience, was almost a pledge. It troubled him much, in the intervals of preparing the materials for the next part of the *Hebrew Grammar*, that he had allowed his sister to die in the hope that he would endeavour to obey her entreaty. This entreaty was, however, beginning to seem less impossible.

The doctor was in no doubt as to the person he should choose as a helpmate. Had not Sarah bidden him marry some loving and tender-hearted woman, who understood the importance of the great work on which he was engaged? And was not Mrs. Firebrace an almost excessively gentle and tender-hearted creature? Had she not shown on all occasions the utmost consideration for himself, and an almost over-appreciation of his humble labours? But, even more than all this, the fact that she was Adelaide's mother drew Nathaniel Simpson to Sophia Firebrace. He had described Adelaide to Mrs. Graham as "a most lovely and gracious young woman;" and the thought of calling her daughter awakened emotions in the heart of the solitary scholar such as no woman had ever awakened there before. The idea of marrying Adelaide had never even crossed his mind. He anxiously debated with himself whether he was not too old to offer himself to so young and elegant a woman as the mother. He would have been inexpressibly shocked if any one had suggested to him that he might think of Adelaide otherwise than as a most dearly loved daughter. His "daughter!" Dr. Simpson had never so much as attempted to write a line of English verse in his life, but it would have taken a very good poet to fairly set down, even in prose, all that this dried-up Doctor of Divinity felt as he said that word to himself.

But it was by very slow degrees that Dr. Simpson began to seriously entertain the idea of matrimony. Ought a man, entirely absorbed in a great work and entirely unused to ordinary social life, to marry? The good doctor answered this question in the negative very decidedly several times over during the first six months after his sister's death; and the keenest observer could have detected infirmity of purpose no otherwise than in the fact that the question and answer were repeated.

The doctor's agreeable impressions of Mrs.
Firebrace were deepened by what he saw of
her at the time of her daughter's marriage.
He soon made a regular habit of dropping into
tea in Queen Anne Street when he left the
Museum, where he was diligently prosecuting
his researches for the notes to his Fifth Part.
On such occasions Adelaide's last letter would
be produced, and the doctor would often surprise the ladies (Charlotte was still with Mrs.
Firebrace) by his knowledge of the places Adelaide described. Once, many years ago, the
doctor had at Mr. Bolland's desire (and
charges) made a three months' tour on the
Continent, and he was a living encyclopædia
so far as classic antiquities were concerned.
Sophia would gladly have heard less of
Thermæ and ampitheatres and inscriptions,
and more of the modern apppearance of the
cities which the doctor described; but she
listened unflinchingly, and only showed that
the effort cost her anything, by putting more
and more green tea into the Indian tea-pot

which her first husband had bought for her in Mysore.

These tea-drinkings, at which Charlotte was extremely absent-minded and might almost have counted for nobody, produced a considerable effect on the minds both of the doctor and of Sophia. The doctor, dropping in thus after an arduous day at the Museum, felt the charm of Sophia's cool drawing-room, and also of Sophia's quiet yet demonstrative welcome. As he looked back on a well-spent day (the results of which lay in a carpet-bag on Mrs. Firebrace's centre table), he would reflect that marriage need interfere no more than these agreeable visits with the great object of his life. Sophia on her side was heartily tired of being a widow ; and her experiences with the major, which she had by no means forgotten, inclined her to look on the irreproachable dignity of Dr. Simpson's position as very desirable, even if a little dull. Even Adelaide did not know of half the humiliations which poor Sophia had endured in her second marriage. If ever she married again, Sophia was resolved that her husband should be a man as much as possible the opposite of the lamented major. Sophia had kept the matter so secret, that she herself had often forgotten it; but there had been a crisis not long before the major's death when only the timely aid of her uncle Lancaster had prevented an execution being put in the house. And at all times, one-half the major's life had been spent in bullying duns, and the other half in contracting new debts—a good many of which were paid by Mr. Lancaster when the major died. Sophia had had more than enough of what she was accustomed to call "rackets." She knew that Dr. Simpson was held in high esteem by persons who would be looked up to by the best society of The Crescent, and she had some time since come to the conclusion that, all things considered, she could not do better. She was shrewd enough to perceive that in the doctor she had neither a good-natured nonentity like her first husband, nor a self-indulgent but tolerably manageable bully like the major, to deal with ; but she was prepared to make some sacrifices for the sake of an assured position. And, lastly, Sophia was well aware that she would appear to great advantage in the somewhat elderly society of scholars and collegiate dons to which the doctor could introduce his wife.

"There must be some very charming ladies at Oxford—now, Dr. Simpson, do confess that there are," said Sophia, daintily extending her little finger as she raised her cup to her lips, and smiled and shook her head in the prettiest way imaginable.

"Doubtless," said the doctor; "but I did not observe it. Decidedly too young a woman, decidedly so," he added, very nearly loud enough for Sophia's sharp ears to hear.

"I can scarcely believe that," said she. "Though, to be sure, you have far more important matters to think of, and I ought to be ashamed of myself for asking such a silly question. But I am not really thoughtless, though I fear I often appear so—it is only my manner. Dear aunt Lancaster always used to say I had such a cheerful disposition ; and people who are of a cheerful disposition often do seem a little thoughtless."

" My dearest madam, believe me, I could never think you thoughtless," said the doctor, as earnestly as Sophia could have desired. Indeed, as she told herself, his manner in saying it was almost as good as a declaration.

CHAPTER XXII.

Hoyst. Howe'er, I'll speak my mind.
The City Madam.

DESPITE these mutually favourable impressions, Dr. Simpson and Mrs. Firebrace parted without coming "to an *éclaircissement*"—to use a favourite expression of Sophia's. The doctor returned to the classic banks of Isis. Mrs. Firebrace went with Charlotte to Riverside House, "to enjoy the luxury of retirement, after their late fatigues," as she informed the doctor. Sophia would have cheerfully consented to enliven her retirement with a little society; but Charlotte (who in her own house behaved, said Sophia, as if she were ten years older than when she was in Queen Anne

Street) said very plainly that it would be painful to her to attempt to renew the scenes of last summer, with all those absent who had made them pleasant. Sophia pondered this speech at her leisure, and came to her own conclusion as to its meaning, much strengthened by Charlotte's love of haunting the gardens of Hampton Court. Upon the whole Sophia was considerably bored by the luxury of retirement, notwithstanding one or two water parties which Charlotte would have gladly refused.

Charlotte spent the autumn days very much alone, dreaming over again all that had happened the summer before, and dreaming also of what might happen when Horace and Adelaide should return. It had been long since arranged that she was to spend a great part of her time with her brother and sister, whether Horace remained at Dockhampton for some years as Mr. Vincent advised, or boldly tried his fortune in London.

Horace had explained to Charlotte all that Vincent had represented to him about the

future of British railways, and had told her
that he had given Vincent *carte blanche* to
make such investments as he judged advisable.
As for Charlotte's own fortune, Horace wished
her to decide for herself.   There was every
probability of Railway Stock rising in value
within the next few years, and even should
there be a fall in the market, Vincent, who had
means of early information, and who thoroughly
understood the whole thing, would be certainly
able to give timely warning.   Still, added
Horace, it was only right to remind her that
the Bank of England must be confessed to be
safer than these new enterprises.

"You are putting your money into them,
Horace?" said Charlotte in her most thoughtful
tone.

"I shall be incurring very great expenses,"
said Horace, "and I owe it to Adelaide not to
lose an opportunity of repairing my certain
losses at Dockhampton—where the legitimate
drama will, I sorely fear, never be sufficiently
supported to pay a manager's expenses."

"I suppose Mr. Vincent knows what is the safest?"

"As to that, you may be quite easy, my dear Charlotte. Dick is to the manner born, and he has friends at Court—I mean at the council board. He does not wish it to be mentioned, but I happen to know for a fact that he has the *very* best authority for all he has told me."

Charlotte desired a little time to think the matter over; and railway projects mingled with more romantic images in the thoughts which made her so dull a companion at Twickenham.

"What on earth are you thinking about, child?" cried Sophia, as Charlotte passed her for the twentieth time. Sophia was sitting at the drawing-room window, reading a novel by Sir Edward Bulwer, and Charlotte was pacing up and down on the garden walk. "You are like those creatures that we saw in Van Amburgh's show. You give me the horrors, child! Come and talk. You've not said a word this hour."

"I might as well tell her," thought Charlotte, "though of course she knows nothing about it."

Sophia however knew enough to go straight to the point in a remarkably short time. So Mr. Vincent had been persuading Horace to put his money into railways? *That* was what he was driving at? But Sophia had always foreseen it. Of course this was why he had worried Horace into quarrelling with his father's lawyers. Ah, if Charlotte's dear father had been alive, this would never have happened! Charlotte would have nothing to do with anything of the kind, if she took Mrs. Firebrace's advice. The poor dear major once put a hundred pounds that he won at a lottery into some railway or other—Sophia forgot the name—but believed it was that very Leeds and Selby, which Charlotte had mentioned. Of course he lost every penny of it, as Mrs. Firebrace had told him he would. And that man Hudson had something to do with it— the linen-draper of York, who, everybody said,

forged his uncle's will.   If Vincent knew him,
as he pretended he did, so much the worse for
Vincent. And if Charlotte thought that putting
her money into these concerns would ever
enable her to help dear Horace carry on his
theatre (Charlotte had hinted at this reason for
not at once choosing the Three per Cents. and
peace of mind), the kindest thing she could do
would be to leave her fortune where it was—
it was safe there.   Mr. Vincent and that man
Hudson were a pair of swindlers, in Sophia's
opinion.   Sophia had never spoken thus plainly
before, out of regard to dear Horace's feelings ;
but this last stroke of Mr. Vincent's policy was
too much—Sophia would be less than a mother
not to speak.   Mr. Vincent had never said he
knew Hudson ?   Then what did he mean by
telling Horace he had the best authority for
knowing which investments to choose ?   And
if he did *not* know Hudson, it was utter folly
for Horace to trust his opinion, clever as he
might be.   Hudson did at least know what he
was about.   Depend upon it, Vincent would

never rest till he had got Horace's fortune
entirely in his own power !

Having said thus much in her first alarm
and wrath, Sophia became aware that she had
been a little indiscreet, and proceeded to beg
Charlotte not to repeat what she had said. "I
was so thankful, my dear girl, when you
refused him," said Sophia, kissing her effu-
sively. "It would have almost broken my
heart to see you sacrificed. But Horace is so
infatuated, and we shall only make him more
obstinate by opposition. We must not interfere *there*. But, for Heaven's sake, don't take
your own money out of the Bank of England ;
the major always said it was like the tortoise—
slow and sure."

On the same day, and at pretty nearly the
same hour, Horace was saying to Adelaide, as
they sat at the window of their hotel, looking
out on the *Boulevard des Italiens*—

"I trust it has some merit ; but the age is
not ripe for a tragedy which attempts to represent the loftier passions."

"I am sure it is a most beautiful tragedy, Horace dear," said Adelaide, stretching out her hand for the roll which Horace held, and from which he had been reading to her his tragedy of *Tarquinius.* "But most actors act so badly. If you could only take all the parts yourself it would be sure to succeed. But I always long to shake Mr. A'Deane—he would spoil anything."

"He thinks he is a powerful actor," said Horace with much scorn; "and the papers praise his facial expression."

"Not the *Post,* Horace dear."

"No; the *Post* goes to the other extreme, and will scarce allow an actor to help out his words by so much as a frown. Poor *Tarquinius!* Well, if Vincent's visions are not mere dreams—and they seem substantial—he shall see the light yet."

CHAPTER XXIII.

'Tis matter of importance.
The cook, sir, is self-will'd.
A New Way to Pay Old Debts.

THE greatest philosophers are not entirely in-
sensible to very humble considerations. Dr.
Simpson went home to Oxford carrying with
him tender thoughts of Adelaide, and very
agreeable reminiscences of her mother ; but
was somewhat sadly persuaded that he would
not know what to do with a wife, even should
Mrs. Firebrace be disposed to make the sacri-
fice of marrying an elderly bachelor. But a
few days at home convinced him that Sarah's
dying advice had been prompted by a fore-
sight and wisdom little less than miraculous.
The unfortunate doctor found his household

at loggerheads, and a general sense of confusion and disorder pervading all his arrangements. His breakfast was unaccountably late ;
there was something wrong in the cooking of
his luncheon. Last, and worst, the housemaid
burst into his study in tears a little before
the hour of dinner, and requested him to
come and speak to Mrs. Swinglesworth. Mrs.
Swinglesworth was a highly respectable widow,
whom Mrs. Graham had procured with much
trouble for the doctor, when he returned from
Bath after Miss Simpson's death.

The doctor was so astounded at this viola-
tion of his sacred territory—into which only
Caleb ever entered to the doctor's knowledge,
and he only at certain times, and on lawful
errands—that he arose without a word, and
followed the sobbing Mary into the kitchen,
where he found Mrs. Swinglesworth engaged
in frying a shoulder of mutton.

"And, please, sir, she've put the fish in
the hoven, and I wouldn't never have disturbed you, if I hadn't ha' bin afraid she'd

set the chimney afire, and Mr. Caleb got a 'oliday to see his nephew and not come back yet, and Mrs. Swinglesworth a-goin' on that strange—— "

During this somewhat incoherent explanation of the housemaid's, Dr. Simpson remained standing in the doorway, apparently striving to comprehend the situation which comprised a good deal of disorder in the furniture and also in Mrs. Swinglesworth's attire.

"Mrs. Swinglesworth"—said the doctor at last, as that good lady continued to frizzle the shoulder of mutton, with very unpleasant results in the way of burnt fat.

Mrs. Swinglesworth turned at the sound of the doctor's voice, and with a sudden and praiseworthy change of intention, seized her frying-pan, and brought it down on the kitchen table with so vigorous a swing that the mutton must have been lodged upon the floor, had it not been by this time stuck too fast to the pan.

"Sir!" exclaimed Mrs. Swinglesworth, with

an attempt at dignity which she was compelled to support with the aid of the table.

"Mrs. Swinglesworth, I am deeply concerned to see you thus," continued the doctor, slowly sawing the air with a sheet of paper which he had forgotten to lay down when thus amazingly summoned. "I beg that you will not attempt to prepare the dinner. You had better take some repose, Mrs. Swinglesworth, and I will speak to you of what has occurred when you are better able to give me your attention."

"If you mean, sir, to insinuate that I am intossicated," said Mrs. Swinglesworth, in a voice which must have irresistibly reminded the doctor of the gyrations described by a drunken man's legs, had he been in the habit of noticing such trivialities, "you're quite mistaken — 'tirely 'staken. Drunk, indeed! R'spect'ble widow woman; never so 'nsulted 'n m' life! No mo' drunk 'n y'are y'rself!"

Mrs. Swinglesworth's speech grew more difficult to report every instant, and an ineffectual effort to cuff Mary's ears completely overset her balance ; luckily, she fell into a chair, and there lay, resting her head on the table and apparently inclined for slumber.

" You had better put the fire out, and leave her till she comes to herself," said the doctor, greatly to Mary's admiration. " And never mind about my dinner. I will take a cup of tea when Caleb comes home."

The doctor's readiness to meet this emergency procured him many sly compliments from his friends ; but how bravely soever he may have borne him, it is certain that he hailed the opportune return of Caleb with the most heartfelt relief, and instantly resigning the conduct of affairs, returned to his study with a very troubled countenance, which only partially cleared when Caleb came an hour later, to inform him that dinner was ready.

" We shouldn't ha' bin so long, sir, but the housekeeper she'd redooced everything to such a quandary as never was," said Caleb as he took his place to wait.

The doctor bent his head and said grace before he answered, "This is a sad affair, Caleb."

"I was afraid it was a-coming to this, sir," said Caleb, briskly whisking off the cover. "We was obliged to brile the salmon, sir. She didn't shut the oven-door, or else it would ha' bin completedly spiled. I've had my suspicions some weeks, sir ; but I wouldn't write to you, sir, not bein' quite so sure as I could wish to be, and not wishin' to perplex your mind, sir."

"It is, indeed, a perplexity, Caleb," said the doctor sighing.

"If I may be so bold, sir, I don't hold with 'ousekeepers, sir. Mr. Bolland, he had a deal o' trouble with 'em at one time an' another."

"I remember that he had, Caleb," said the doctor sighing again.

The doctor had an interview with Mrs. Swinglesworth next day, in the course of which she wept much and promised amendment, alleging, in excuse for her misdeeds, that "she had seen better days," and "had never ex-

pected to come down to be a housekeeper."
The late Mr. Swinglesworth having been a
respectable builder in a small way, some persons may not sympathize with his relict's
sense of degradation. But things are to us
as we feel them to be; and may not a builder's
widow, reduced to keep house for a Doctor of
Divinity, feel a pang as great as an ex-chan-
cellor's dame regretting the business of the
nation?

The doctor "was worked upon" (to quote
Caleb) to try Mrs. Swinglesworth once more;
but the discovery of that respectable woman in
his study, looking as she said for the rolling-
pin, and dropping the tallow from a lighted
candle among his papers, sealed her fate—and,
ultimately the doctor's.

In attempting to describe the events of
several nearly connected lives, a chronicler is
often puzzled as to how much he may leave
out. All our lives are full of incident, as every
drop of water in a river is full of motion; but
lives differ as vastly as rivers in the scenery

through which they pass, and no two leagues
of meadow are alike—but that is a master-
hand indeed which can so paint the level leas
that the beholder forgets to long for crag and
cataract. Nor is distrust of his own powers
the sole difficulty which besets the chronicler.
He often does not know which are the important events in the lives he is recording, and
which may be omitted as of no permanent
bearing on the story ; for the closer he looks
into his own life and the lives of those whom
he has known best, the smaller seem the links
in the chain of circumstance, and the more
does he perceive that causes are constant and
not intermittent. If this had not been, that had
not been ; if that had not been, the other had
not been. Thus to-day looks back and reproaches yesterday, and yesterday accuses the
day before; and *if,* like Ariadne's clew, takes us
quite through life's labyrinth from end to end.
We are influenced by each other, and we pay
back the debt with usury, like those planets
whose entangled courses in some sort prevent

the very chaos they threaten. We are changed, and we in our turn change those who have changed us.

Mrs. Firebrace was not in the habit of thus generalizing her impressions, but no one had a clearer perception of particular instances of this, as of most other facts affecting the characters of her friends and acquaintances; and in the week which Horace and Adelaide spent at Twickenham on their return from the Continent she made many mental and a few verbal comments on the good which Addy had already done Horace. He appeared to Mrs. Firebrace to have "less nonsense about him," and to be more like other people. Addy, as Sophia was pleased to see, had grown much less shy, and had acquired a quiet self-possession and matronly dignity, from which her mother augured well.

"I don't doubt, child, that you'll be able to manage Horace very well," she said one day to Adelaide, as they were sitting on a seat in the garden. "Mr. Vincent is your chief difficulty. I have got Charlotte to hear reason; but I suppose you know that Horace is letting him have his way in everything. Don't you let him meddle with your own little fortune— it's not much, to be sure, but it will always be pin-money for you. And of course Horace will give up this ridiculous theatre of his, if you go the right way to work. I'm glad now that he *was* so obstinate about the house in Russell Square. It's not exactly in a fashionable quarter, but it *is* a town house, and that's something. This crotchet won't last long ; and, with Horace's splendid fortune, there's hardly anything he mightn't rise to, if he went into Parliament."

" Horace would rather reform the drama, mamma, than go into Parliament. He does not care much for politics," said Adelaide. " And, oh, he has written such a splendid tragedy ! "

" Splendid fiddlestick ! " exclaimed Sophia. " Addy, I do hope you won't be such a fool as to encourage him to squander any more of his

money on this folly. I can't think how it is
you have no ambition. You are a very elegant
young woman, and with Horace's fortune and
connection and the position he might easily
take, you might be quite a leader of *tong*. But
what with Horace flinging his money away at
the theatre, and Mr. Vincent making ducks
and drakes of it in railways, and you without
a spark of proper spirit—I declare I'm provoked !——My dearest Horace, I was just
telling Addy that you have turned her into
quite an elegant young woman !"

CHAPTER XXIV.

He and his principles are out of fashion.
Lord and Lady Russell.

ADELAIDE was perfectly contented with the unpretending house which Horace had prepared for her in Dockhampton. She entered heart and soul into all the business of the theatre, and was never too tired or too busy to listen to Horace's account of the day's events. Into her attentive and sympathetic ear he poured his complaints, his hopes, and his disappointments. He even occasionally consulted her as to the mode of delivering a speech which he wished to render unusually effective. She knew of the quarrels in the green-room, and the deficiencies in the ex-

chequer—at neither of which did she so much
as hint in her letters to her mother. The
much-harassed manager could tell Adelaide of
his troubles, and never even suspect her of
disloyalty to his ambition.

"I have been reading about some of the
great actors, Horace dear," she said to him
one day, when he returned from a morning
rehearsal of *The Honeymoon*, at which Miss
Annesley had been outrageously rude to
Kiddle; "and they all seem to have been
worried dreadfully. I am sure Mrs. Cibber
was quite as tiresome as Miss Annesley."

"But she *could* act if she liked," said
poor Horace. "Miss Annesley is a pretty
vivacious creature; but she does not respond
to my efforts to impart dignity to the characters we represent. She drags me down,
Adelaide! I shall never rise to the full scope
of my powers in the provinces. I shall never
be properly supported by a provincial cast.
I do not expect a Mrs. Siddons; I only ask
not to be made ridiculous by a pert actress,

who is utterly incapable of the sustained effort necessary for tragedy."

Theodore Paston had returned. He was working very hard, and seldom found time to call on Adelaide. It was commonly reported among the company that Mr. Paston was writing an opera; but if so, he had not mentioned the fact to the manager.

"Our enterprising manager," as the *Post* continued to call him, often felt the harness gall him terribly. "Kiddle," he exclaimed, in the midst of a discussion on the Christmas piece, "I have been steadily going downhill ever since I took the theatre!"

"You hadn't hardly ought to say that, Mr. Lancaster," replied Kiddle. "I'm sure, with the exception of the first week or two, our receipts have been larger of late than they ever was."

"I don't mean the money—that is not my first consideration, as you very well know. I mean that we have been steadily lowering our standard to suit the public taste."

"Must do it, Mr. Lancaster. Must hit the public taste, sir, must a manager, or he's lost."

"Then let him be lost!" said Horace, with his tragedy voice. "It seems to me," he continued, fretfully, "that the public taste itself grows more and more corrupt. We have gradually come down from *Hamlet* and *The School for Scandal* to *George Barnwell* and *The Honeymoon.*"

"*George Barnwell* was only put on on an emergency. And many a play ain't had near such a run as *George Barnwell*," said Kiddle, reflectively. "It's always safe to fall back on *George Barnwell.*"

"The coarsest melodrama!" said Horace, his eyes involuntarily wandering to *Tarquinius* which lay on the table. He turned over the first page with a very audible sigh.

"There's merit, I don't doubt, in that play of yours, Mr. Lancaster," said Kiddle, observing the manager however somewhat doubtfully. "But if you'll be advised by me, you

won't bring it out now—nor, I should say,
here."

"*Damon and Pythias* did very well."

"The novelty carried it off. Yes; we did
pretty well," said Kiddle, still eyeing *Tarquinius* askance, and adding after a few
moments' pause, during which Horace gazed
silently at the open page of his unappreciated
tragedy, "Culpepper would like *Damon and
Pythias* to be played for his benefit.

There had been a little difficulty about this
matter, Mr. Culpepper rather naturally wishing to take a prominent part on his benefit
night. Mr. Culpepper had even been heard
to say that it "was devilish hard that he must
choose between wearing a sheet" (thus did
he designate that august garment, the Dorian
tunic), "and taking a part so small, you
couldn't see it without a telescope." For Mr.
Culpepper had never ceased to resent what he
called the manager's "usurpation" of all the
good parts. *Damon*, however, was a principal
part, and the play had taken. Mr. Cul-

pepper had hesitated between this play and
The School for Scandal; but the manager
had, when that piece was put on in the preceding season, made his *Charles* so unwarrant-
ably prominent (having indeed, said the *Post*,
so wrought out the woes of that amiable
prodigal, as to throw an almost tragic intensity
into the part), that he finally decided on
Damon and Pythias, "where," as he remarked
to Miss Annesley, "his own name came first
in the bill, at any rate."

In arriving at this decision, Mr. Culpepper
helped unconsciously to influence the des-
tinies of several persons of whom he knew
little or nothing.

Mrs. Firebrace, whom Adelaide kept duti-
fully informed of everything except the
manager's troubles, suggested that dear Addy
should invite Dr. Simpson to spend Christmas
at Dockhampton, so timing his visit as to
ensure his seeing *Damon and Pythias*, which
as a classic drama he would so highly appreciate. Adelaide, whose reverence for the

doctor had ceased to be painful, wrote accordingly, and somewhat to her surprise the
doctor accepted her invitation.   Long before
he came, Sophia had made up her mind that
a visit to the house of a theatrical manager—
at least of one so engrossed as Horace—might
be very well for a time, but the time was apt
to hang rather heavy.   How Adelaide could
endure it, Sophia could not understand.   She
supposed that if Addy had chosen, she could
have got together a little circle, and seen a
little society, though Horace *was* for ever-
lasting acting, or rehearsing, or studying new
parts, or having his life worried out of him
by that odious Mr. Kiddle, who seemed to
think that Horace was to be always at his
beck and call.   Mr. Paston was presuming
enough, or had been—he was decidedly im-
proved; but he, Sophia supposed, was a
gentleman, while as for this Mr. Kiddle—— !
But what with Horace a perfect slave to the
theatre, and Addy a perfect slave to Horace,
and Horace so monstrous proud that he never

could see that his position was likely to be a barrier——

. "Horace does not care to know people who look down upon him because he is an actor, mamma," said Adelaide, to whom Sophia had spoken a very small piece of her mind on the whole subject of Horace's enterprise.

"If I had had the least idea that he would be so wrapped up in his theatre as all this, I never would have given my consent to your marriage, Addy. You are buried alive here, in this poky little house. You might as well be the wife of a poor, strolling player; you couldn't be more of a slave! I declare Horace thinks of nothing else—positively of nothing! If I had not thought that he would come to his senses when he was married—or, at any rate, come to London—the eccentricities of a man of Horace's fortune don't matter so much in town, but he ought to know that here they *are* a barrier. I'm sure I often wish you had accepted Captain Overton."

"Mamma! Captain Overton never asked me—and if he had——"

" You would have refused him. You always were a fool, Addy! Where you got it from, *I* don't know! And as for Captain Overton's not asking you, every one could see he admired you ; and it is very bad taste for a young woman to go about saying a man never asked her. Of course, you needn't say that he did. He would have asked you if you had not been so distant with him ; and I'm sure I'm very sorry—— "

Adelaide walked out of the room at this point of the conversation, or Sophia might have forgotten her usual discretion still further.

Dr. Simpson talked chiefly during his visit of the Greek drama, with an *excursus* or two on the Roman. Mr. Kiddle, who happened to come in at the end of one of the doctor's conversations with Horace on this topic, was fairly aghast at the learning displayed on both sides ; and remarked to Mrs. Kiddle on his return, that it was no wonder Mr. Lancaster was so hard to manage (*Quis custodiet ipsos*

custodes?) if he knew all these out-of-the-
way things, and had his head as full as all
this of the Greeks and Romans. The good
doctor was, it must be confessed, a little
overwhelming. He assisted at the representation of *Damon and Pythias*, with a total
oblivion of the modern stage, very edifying
to Mr. Paston, accustomed to learned Ger-
mans, but perplexing to the barbaric English
provincial mind. The doctor watched the
performers with a solemn classic attention,
and needed but his academic robes to have
looked like his own statue. Between the
acts, he favoured the ladies with many
learned remarks, and he was so obliging as
to compliment Horace on his fidelity to
classic tradition.

"So far, of course," added the doctor
conscientiously, "as is possible in a representation which in many material points, departs
so widely—although, as I am aware, unavoid-
ably—from what we know of the Greek form
of the drama."

" The public is a tyrannous master, Dr. Simpson," said Horace. " I find it often a thankless task to endeavour to uphold the dignity of the stage."

" Nay, I suppose," said the doctor (looking terribly like his statue), " that the Athenians —who were in some respects a volatile people —indulged in some amount of buffoonery. We find many allusions to comic actors—and Homer himself, in introducing Thersites into an heroic poem——"

It was on this occasion that Mr. Kiddle was so profoundly impressed by Horace's scholarship as well-nigh to despair of him as the manager of an English theatre.

In the course of his visit, the doctor confided some of his domestic difficulties to Mrs. Firebrace's sympathizing ear, comprehending however Mrs. Swinglesworth's delinquencies under the brief statement that his housekeeper, " an otherwise respectable woman, had unfortunately contracted intemperate habits," and entering into no details.

Sophia, who doated on details, put a strong
constraint upon herself and asked no questions, but was only shocked to hear that the
doctor's literary work had been somewhat
interrupted by these sad delinquencies on the
part of those who should have made it their
study to spare him all unnecessary worry.

"Of course," said Sophia, wiping a tear
from her eye (Sophia's eyes swam in actual
tears on the slightest provocation)—"of
course, dear doctor, servants can never *quite*
supply the place which——"

"Ah, my dear madam, your keen perception
guides you, as usual, to the root of the
matter," said the doctor mournfully.

"I should like to ask you a question,
doctor," said Sophia, with a charming hesitation, but without the least embarrassment.
"But I have no right—it would be too great
a liberty. And yet I have sometimes thought
that some one ought to suggest it to you."

"Pray speak without the slightest hesitation, my dear madam. Any question you

ask can only be dictated by the kindest motives."

"Well, then, doctor, have you never—pray forgive me—but have you never thought that you might be the happier for a wife to look after your interests, and take all care off your hands? You must know many ladies at Oxford." Sophia said this with an admirable combination of delicacy and decision, as of one certain that her advice is sound, but having no possible interest in the matter either way.

The doctor grew very red. "My dear madam," he began—

"Now I have offended you, I know!" cried Sophia.

"My dear madam, nothing could be farther from my thoughts," said the doctor. "But what right have I to ask any lady to become my wife? I am no longer a young man—I might almost call myself an old one—I have lived more among books than men, and I have devoted my life to a work which will engross all my energies, and most of my thoughts, so long as it shall please God to grant me the use of my faculties. I cannot —indeed, I am fixedly determined not to alter my manner of life, which has long been that of a recluse."

"No one worthy of you would wish it or allow it," said Sophia. Sophia laid aside most of her little airs and graces when she talked with the doctor, for whom she was beginning to feel as much respect as her nature was capable of. "Any wife worthy of you would be too proud of your fame to wish to stand in your way."

The doctor's fame, Sophia reflected, was of an eminently respectable kind, and involved none of the discomforts which Horace and Addy seemed quite to enjoy, but which only recalled the major to Sophia's mind.

"Could I think that I might ask a lady to become my wife on such terms?" said the doctor.

"Try, doctor, try. A great deal is lost for want of asking," said Sophia with a coquettish toss of her head which she could not quite repress. "Indeed, I have felt for you. I know, by sad experience, what it is to be left alone in the world."

Sophia added this with very real emotion. The major had caused her a deal of trouble both before and after he left her a disconsolate widow.

The doctor got up, and went to the window; then he came back to the little table at which Sophia was sitting. But he turned again to the window without speaking, and Sophia netted a few more meshes of the curtain she was making. Sophia had a very neat foot, and netted a good deal.

At last the doctor came back again to the table. "Sophia," he said, "you embolden me to ask whether you yourself will accept all that I have to offer you, on such conditions as I have explained to you? Do not answer hastily. Such a step should not be taken lightly; nor is either of us free to consider ourselves alone in the matter. But I wish

to assure you that I shall ever regard Adelaide
as my daughter, and that I shall ever take as
deep an interest in all which concerns her as
though she were my own child."

CHAPTER XXV.

If she and I be pleas'd, what's that to you ?
Taming of the Shrew.

IT is wonderful how quickly Time runs on
with us, when once he has got his wheel into
a rut.   Even a somewhat uncomfortable rut
helps him along in a surprising degree.   The
routine of a prison serves to pass the time
quicker than is supposed, if we may judge
from the revelations of ingenious felons.
Routine is an inclined plane, down which the
wheels of Time roll faster and faster.   While
we are very young, and unused to living, Time
goes slowly with us ; but even the schoolboy
finds Saturday afternoon coming round very
soon, after the first week or two of the new
term.

This truth applies chiefly, of course, to persons who take their regular meals, and live orderly lives. But, in time, almost everything —from the dribbling of a water-spout to the explosion of a bomb—grows monotonous, and produces some of the effects of regularity.

Adelaide's life was decidedly irregular, but even with her the months began to fly; while as for the days, they seemed gone directly. There was a good deal of excitement about the Queen's marriage. The town was illuminated. Horace gave a free performance, which at least proved that there were people enough in Dockhampton to fill the theatre. Mr. Vincent wrote frequently, and came down now and then. Horace was aware that there was an understanding between him and Amelia Overton, but the engagement was not openly declared. Sir John had had a fit of apoplexy, brought on, Vincent believed, by wrath at the presentation of Mr. Owen to the Queen. Mr. Copeland, whose interest in politics had revived since

the branch line from Cloppingford was talked
of in such earnest, did not think of resigning
just yet, but was in very poor health, and
would willingly have kept Mr. Vincent employed in going between him and the railway
wire-pullers. Vincent was, however, making
his way, and many others besides Sir John
now looked on him as a rising young man.

Adelaide's condition opportunely prevented
her being present at her mother's marriage.
She had much astonished Sophia by bursting
into tears when she first heard of the doctor's
proposal.

"You're an incomprehensible child, Addy,"
said Sophia. "You can but just remember
your poor father; and, as for the major, I'm
sure no one could expect I should remain a
widow for his sake! And I have never seen
a man whom I respect so highly as I do
Dr. Simpson. I wonder you don't feel it an
honour."

"My dear," said the doctor, when he saw
Adelaide after the announcement, and speak-

ing with a new fatherly familiarity in his voice
and manner, "*she* desired it."

The doctor touched, with that scholarly
crooked fore-finger of his, an antique ring,
which had once been Mr. Bolland's, and which
Sarah Simpson had requested should be given
to Adelaide. Sophia thought it an old-
fashioned thing; but Adelaide always wore it.

Sophia was married with great quiet and
decorum from her house in Queen Anne
Street. Mr. Hillyard, who had given Adelaide
a silver service on her own marriage, wrote to
say that it would not be fair not to serve the
mother the same as the daughter; and boldly
asked permission to give the bride away.
Whether this brilliant stroke of policy ema-
nated from "plain G. H.'s" own brain, or
was suggested by his mischievous daughter
Sophy, who thus devised a kind of poetical
justice on Mrs. Firebrace (whose manœuvres
at Adelaide's wedding had been clearly seen
through by that quick-witted young woman),
is uncertain; but probabilities incline to the

latter theory, especially as Sophy's own wits
were now reinforced by those of a young
barrister on the western circuit, to whom she
had lately contracted herself. Be this as it
may, Sophia accepted the silver service, and
Mr. Hillyard gave her away. After all, a
silver tea-service is a consideration, when one's
late husband has run through so much as did
the major ; and a drysalter may, as Sophia
justly remarked, be a very respectable man.

Sophia and the doctor did not take a
wedding trip. Dr. Simpson's work had suffered several interruptions ; and perhaps
Sophia herself thought that a *tête-à-tête* tour
might be a little dull. At any rate, she went
to Oxford with a very good grace, and set the
doctor's household in order in no time. She
made herself agreeable to Caleb, and had her
own way with every one else. It was a part
of Sophia's character to accept a situation.
Unless under very exceptional provocation, she
never offended any one—or, at least, any one
of any influence. She perceived at a glance

that Caleb was as immovable a fact of her
future as the doctor himself, and she made the
best of the fact. She also perceived at once
that Caleb would guard the doctor's interests
with a lynx eye; and, instead of resenting
this, as a person of less *savoir vivre* might
have done, she resolved at once to flatter
Caleb and save herself some trouble, by en-
couraging him to look after the doctor as much
as he chose, and in his own way. Perhaps,
had Caleb been the late Mr. Bolland's confidential housekeeper instead of his confidential
butler and valet, Sophia might have found
her philosophy put more shrewdly to the test;
but as it was, Caleb himself was heard to say
that it was a good thing on the whole that
Miss Sarah had left it in her will that the
doctor was to marry, for a mistress could keep
the women in better order than a master could,
especially when he was a scholar like the
doctor.

To do her justice, Sophia certainly secured
the doctor much more undisturbed quiet than

he had enjoyed since his sister's death. It was not to be expected that a charming and elegant woman, not much over forty, should "immure herself"—a favourite phrase of Sophia's. And of course, she received many wedding calls, all of which she returned, and which formed the foundation of a by no means despicable social edifice, which she managed in an incredibly short time (to the doctor) to raise on her own behoof. She gave quiet little kettledrums, and even a few receptions, at which latter the doctor usually showed for a few minutes. The doctor was not disturbed by his wife's visitors. Sophia took the precaution to have double doors made to his study; and the distant strains of the harp or pianoforte, if they ever penetrated his sanctum, did not seriously annoy him. And it must be carefully remembered that Sophia's society was of the most select order—altogether unexceptional, as she wrote to Adelaide—none of those half-pay people, who never, somehow, seem *quite* satisfactory. Sophia was a more

voluminous correspondent than ever since the
Penny Post had been established. Adelaide
received one of Mr. Mulready's envelopes
every week.

Various smaller excitements broke the
monotony of the strife between the legitimate drama, represented by Horace, and the
illegitimate drama, represented by Mr. Kiddle.
Two or three public events gave occasion
for special performances. And Mr. Vincent's
affairs were not unexciting, to say nothing of
the railway projects, the mysterious interest
of which Adelaide felt, without as yet quite
knowing why. She carefully kept all allusions
to this subject out of her letters to her mother,
who still from time to time threw out hints
about Addy's beginning to have an opinion of
her own.

But the year was chiefly marked to Adelaide
by the birth of her son. He was obliging
enough to be born in time for her to be con-
valescent by August, when Horace closed the
theatre, and took a two months' holiday. It

was spent, at Charlotte's eager entreaty, at
Riverside House; and here a very happy party
assembled in the pleasant autumn weather.
Sophia was there, and, to Caleb's utter amaze-
ment, the doctor also. Caleb's organ of
wonder had a good deal of exercise about this
time. The doctor had expressed a great wish
to stand sponsor to Adelaide's child, and had
actually put some pages of the *Hebrew
Grammar* in his pocket to revise by the way
—but more to persuade himself that he was
losing no time, for he went over them all again
when he returned, much to Caleb's distress at
this waste of labour—and had gone down to
Dockhampton with Sophia, who was to be
godmother. Sophia was vexed, but not surprised, to find that Mr. Vincent was the other
godfather. She held her peace however for
that time; but when the whole party was
assembled at Twickenham, she took an opportunity one sultry afternoon, as they all (except
Adelaide) sat watching the approach of a
thunderstorm, to observe that she must own

she should be very uneasy if dear, darling Addy's sweet little boy had not at least one godfather who would attend properly to his religious principles.

"I would not pain you for the world, my dear Horace," said Sophia (her remarks were made *à propos* of some mention of Vincent, who was expected that evening); "but I *have* sometimes wondered a little at your extreme partiality for a person who is, I fear, very little better than a free-thinker."

"Indeed!" said Dr. Simpson. "I am sorry to hear this of so accomplished a person as Mr. Vincent appears to be."

"I do not think, sir," said Horace, "that any one would be justified in calling Vincent a free-thinker. Indeed, Sophia, you have never done him justice; believe me, you have not. Great intellectual brilliancy, such as his, sometimes gives an appearance of undervaluing more serious subjects. Vincent is a man to profess less than he believes—I grant that; and I do not mind telling you,

Sophia, that I have sometimes wished he were less given to underrate his own faith. But I think the study of the law tends to extreme caution of expression, and Vincent speaks of religion no otherwise than he does of every other subject into which the imagination enters. Vincent is the most consistent man I know."

CHAPTER XXVI.

Cade. There shall be, in England, seven halfpenny loaves sold for a penny.—*2nd Part of King Henry VI.*

IT has been said so often that happiness has no history, that we may easily accept the saying too literally, and forget one or two modifying facts which most proverbs require to make them more than skin-deep true. No life is without movement of some kind or other; the happiest nation on earth could record change and excitement. If it was vexed by no wars or revolutions, it at least knew alternating seasons—fair weather and storms, bad harvests and plenteous years, with an eclipse and a comet or so now and then, to remind it of the vaster calamities that earth is heir to. But even on the fairest summer day, the stream flows on, and the happiest year has its history; though it may be that ears which are too dull to catch notes less piercing than trumpet-calls, may not heed the subtler harmonies of peace and repose.

Thus, in the least eventful period of Horace's life, his days were so full of bustle and excitement, that he chafed at the little leisure left him by his duties, and often bitterly complained to Adelaide that he had time neither to study his parts, nor to perfect his tragedies. He repeated a hundred times, that he was resolved to remain in Dockhampton not a week longer than should be necessary to establish a sufficient reputation for him to command a London audience.

"It is all very well to talk about commanding a London audience, Mr. Lancaster," Kiddle would say, whenever he heard Horace talk in this fashion. "But there's no one as *can* be sure of a London house. They know what's what, d—— 'em, and you can't put 'em off with cheap scenery. A provincial pit will always clap spangles and blue fire, but the Londoners want it all real, or next door to it."

"My Christmas pieces cost more than they bring me," answered Horace to this reasoning of Kiddle's.

"Nothing to what you'd have to do in London, take my word for it, Mr. Lancaster. They've been spoiled, have the Londoners, till they're that d—d critical, they'd pick holes in the Queen's State coach." Mr. Kiddle also threw a deal of cold water on the tragedy, the dialogue of which he pronounced to be heavier than Shakespeare's. "If you'll be ruled by my advice, Mr. Lancaster, you'll stick to the old pieces just at first."

"Just at first!" exclaimed Horace, out of patience. "I have had this theatre two years already!"

"And what's two years to learn a business like ours in, Mr. Lancaster? And I doubt you hadn't hardly seen as much as the inside of a green-room till you played at Bristol! Don't you try to play to a London audience yet awhile—more especially as you take the tragic line."

When Mr. Kiddle gave this unpalatable advice to the manager, the mounting tide of Mr. Vincent's fortunes had left him safely stranded in Parliament. Mr. Copeland's revived energies had begun to flag again under several severe attacks of gout, and he much preferred busying himself in a desultory way as an amateur railway projector, to assisting ever so harmlessly at the councils of the nation. Mr. Copeland had been an M.P. long enough to discover that he was not suited for the patient drudgery of committees. He was one of those men who are by nature *dilettanti*, and who can work harder at anything than at the obvious duties of their position. His really precarious health aggravated, but did not produce, this tendency. He had some natural bent towards mechanics, and might, had he

been born a comparatively poor man, have
become a respectable civil engineer; and his
growing interest in railways was only the
latest development of a life-long hobby. It
was now his great ambition to be a railway director—but a director who should
chiefly concern himself with the actual
engineering operations of the company. He
understood very little, and cared less, about
the financial part of a director's functions,
but for this he trusted implicitly to Vincent.
When, therefore, anti-corn law meetings,
railways, electric telegraphs, and many other
signs of the times more or less conspicuous,
brought the country to a general election, Mr.
Copeland resolved not to stand again, but to
bring in in his stead his gifted young friend, who
would fight the battles of the railways with
youthful vigour, and would do pretty much as
Mr. Copeland desired him. He had not much
trouble in securing Vincent's return—the
speech which the new candidate made from
the window of the *Overton Arms*, setting

forth the advantages of railways, having brought the matter down to the comprehension of the poorest of the free and independent electors assembled in Cloppingford market-place. Cloppingford not being on the high road, Mr. Vincent's task was rendered somewhat easier, as he had not much coaching interest to talk down ; but he gave them an eloquent description of the traffic between Southampton and London, before and after the opening of the railway ; and so effectually pleaded the cause of the iron road, that he left a good many of the electors under the pleasing delusion that only a railway was wanting to make Cloppingford as important a place as Birmingham or Manchester.

"The poorest piece of land becomes as valuable at the most fertile, when the iron coach is driven across it," exclaimed Vincent, throwing out his arm as it were across half the world. " A hundred miles become as ten, so much is distance lessened ; one day becomes as three—as three ? nay, as seven—so much is time saved by this most happy application of science to the wants of mankind! A journey by coach is expensive, slow, inconvenient——"

"How about that 'ere accident t'other day, master?" asked a man in the crowd.

"Have there been no accidents to stage-coaches?" said Vincent, instantly singling out the man who had interrupted him. "I wonder a sensible-looking fellow like you should let yourself be carried away by prejudice. Accidents happen everywhere. A man was killed here last week, by a fall from the scaffolding of Mr. Perry's house; but I suppose no one thinks Mr. Perry ought not to have had his house new roofed?" This local allusion had a great effect on the crowd, which hereupon cheered lustily.

"Mr. Copeland has been a great benefactor to this town," continued Vincent. "Whatever I may be able to do for you, should you send me to Parliament, will be only the continuation of the work he has begun. I have had the good fortune to be thrown into contact with some of the great railroad men up in London, and I have perhaps learned a little from them; but it was Mr. Copeland who first thought of getting a railroad for Cloppingford, and I hope you will always remember it, when Cloppingford is an important town, with a score of factory chimneys, where now there is one; and I hope several of the new streets which are sure to be built as soon as the railroad is opened, will be named after Mr. Copeland and Sir John Overton, and the other gentlemen who have laboured for the good of the town. Depend upon it, gentlemen, railways are going to be the making or the marring of every town in the country. Those towns which have not got the public spirit and enterprise to keep pace with the times, will be left in the lurch, and will see their trade and manufactures deserting them for their more clear-sighted neighbours—they will be marred by the new railroads. Those towns which have the pluck and the shrewdness to be beforehand with the times, will find themselves

centres of commerce and manufacture; through
them will pour the enriching tides of traffic;
they will be on the high-ways of England,
while their foolish neighbours will be left in
deserted by-ways. Such towns will be made
by the very railroad which has half ruined
their short-sighted neighbours, who would not
move on with the times, and so will have been
left behind by the times. Such a centre,
gentlemen, it shall be my endeavour, should
you return me, to make this industrious
and flourishing borough of Cloppingford."

Sir John Overton, who stood by Mr. Vincent,
but who fortunately did not hear any one
connected sentence of this progressive speech,
shook Mr. Vincent by the hand in face of
all the people when he concluded. Sir John
had interest at Cloppingford scarcely second
to Mr. Copeland, whom he had always warmly
supported. As for that gentleman, he waved
his hat enthusiastically, and shook Vincent's
hand at frequent intervals all the rest of the
day.

Mr. Vincent was, of course, put forward in the Tory interest; but there was virtually no opposition—a certain Whig attorney, who had been asked to stand by the few electors of the opposite colour, having been nowhere at all at the show of hands. A poll was not even demanded, and Richard Vincent, Esq., was declared duly returned for the borough of Cloppingford. Mr. Copeland insisted on defraying the expenses of the election, which were not large—chiefly consisting in the hire of rooms at the *Overton Arms,* and in the printing of sundry placards on paper of the deepest blue, which were affixed to every available wall, post, shed, and pump in the borough. These placards called Mr. Vincent a supporter of Sir Robert Peel, but enlarged much more on the advantages he would procure for Cloppingford. "VINCENT AND THE BRITISH CONSTITUTION" was cast entirely into the shade by "VINCENT AND A RAILROAD FOR CLOPPINGFORD."

Mr. Vincent had spoken in unqualified terms of the prospects of the great enterprises which were so soon to change not only the outward aspects of the country, but also to work a vast alteration in all which goes to make the life of a people. But there was a temporary depression in the market, and Horace had resisted all Vincent's persuasions to allow him to buy any more shares in railway stock. Horace mentioned the matter to Adelaide, who agreed with him that it was better not to incur certain risk and anxiety for an uncertain advantage. Mr. Copeland however was more sanguine, or, perhaps, less averse to a little of the excitement of gambling. Vincent put him in the way of buying a large number of Leeds and Selby shares, with which company Vincent was understood to be officially connected, though no one knew exactly in what capacity.

Horace's interest in all these events was of the most vicarious sort. In politics, he was decidedly opposed to his friend—if, indeed, the manager of the Dockhampton Theatre could be said to have any politics. Horace had a gentlemanly aversion to Chartists, but he desired the repeal of the duties on corn, and was for toleration and liberal-mindedness in all things outside the domain of art, within which he was as uncompromisingly exclusive as Sir John was in politics. Horace voted on the Liberal side, but he was not vitally interested in the election nor in the petition against the return, and he rejoiced in Vincent's election none the less because Vincent was a Tory. He wrote to the new member, imparting a few warnings concerning railway shares which his friend, the editor of the *Post*, had just been urging on him, and advising Vincent to lose no time in pressing his suit with Amelia Overton. Mr. Vincent took this latter piece of advice so much to heart (or had perhaps resolved on his course already), that before the " Do-nothing Parliament " was prorogued in October, Sir John had accepted him as a son-in-law.

"And, demmy, my lady," said Sir John, commenting to his spouse on the betrothal, "if I don't think Vincent's the best of the bunch. Bingham's a clever fellow in his way, but Vincent can talk his head off any day. And as for Fidelle, the fellow's an ass—though, to be sure, I believe he's managed somehow or other to get the whip-hand of Blanche; how he's done it, Lord only knows. But he can't hold a candle to Vincent. Vincent will make his fortune, and, now that our side's in, he'll be made a judge before he can say 'Jack Robinson.'"

CHAPTER XXVII.

You read Shakespeare! Get Cocker's Arithmetic;
you may buy it for a shilling on any stall—best book
that ever was wrote.—*The Apprentice.*

ALTHOUGH possessed of several important quali-
fications for dramatic success, Mr. Lancaster
was too much of the fine gentleman to make
a business-undertaking answer. This was
Mr. Kiddle's opinion, formed at first sight,
and confirmed as time went on. One never
knew where to have Mr. Lancaster; not that
he could be called unpunctual, in the ordinary
sense of the term—never had Mr. Kiddle (nor
Mrs. Kiddle either) been connected with a
theatre in which Saturday night was so strictly
observed. But the fact remained that one
never knew where to have Mr. Lancaster. As

if his notions about the legitimate were not enough to ruin any three managers, he was always going yet further out of his way to lessen his receipts. He shut the theatre when the news came of the disasters in Cabul, and put up a notice to the effect that, "in consequence of the calamitous news received from Afghanistan, there will be no representation to-night."

"It's all very well to say it ain't decent to open the theatre," said the much-enduring Kiddle to his spouse—whose naturally ample person had increased with each succeeding year, until it had reached a degree of *embonpoint* which made it out of the question for her to attempt *Belvidera;* "but if *Hamlet* or *Othello* had been on, he'd have played. It's only the comedies he's so ready to put off."

Mr. Culpepper shared this opinion of the stage manager's, and observed to A'Deane that any one could see with half an eye that Lancaster never lost an opportunity of cutting him (Culpepper) out of a part which suited him.

Mr. A'Deane, having had the misfortune the night before to stumble against some object (nature not ascertained, but believed to be a lamp-post) on his way home, whereby he had received a black eye of the most pronounced character, and being, moreover, " out of sorts " this morning, chose to consider the expression Mr. Culpepper had used as a premeditated insult, and replied shortly, that " half an eye or a whole one, he was eternally beatified if he did not think Mr. Culpepper an ungrateful beast, to speak thus of a manager who never docked their salaries, however many off-nights he gave. For his part, Mr. A'Deane fully agreed with the manager that it would be disgusting to be acting a farce on the top of the news from India." So saying, A'Deane turned abruptly on his heel—in that very manner which always brought down the gallery, when he played *Claudius* of Denmark, and departed,

"to try and get his eye right by to-morrow—
and his temper, too," as Culpepper said with
a sneer to Miss Annesley and Miss Elton,
to whom he narrated the conversation.

The troubles of a manager are sometimes
amusing reading, but in practice, they have
a tendency to pall upon their subject, especially if he aspires to the higher glories of
his profession. Horace chafed all the more,
because he cherished an ambition, known to
none but his wife, his sister, and Richard
Vincent, of being, like the great poet whom
he personally resembled, both actor and
author. He had employed every moment of
leisure in composition, and had planned and
partly written half-a-dozen tragedies, most of
them founded on incidents in classic history.
Adelaide greatly admired these productions—
for which she had sometimes made very
useful suggestions—but was inclined to regret
their tragic terminations, and had entreated
Horace to write a play which should end well,
and which should have more love in it.

Charlotte agreed with her; while Vincent (to whom Horace had read *Camillus* and *Jugurtha*) remarked that these plays would certainly have had a great run two hundred years ago.

Vincent had been down at Dockhampton very often of late, and had twice brought Amelia, who was delighted and astonished at everything, and whose admiration of her husband's talents might have awakened Adelaide's jealousy on behalf of Horace, if Amelia had been less simple-minded in her exaltation of her Richard.

"Mr. Lancaster need not be at all anxious about the theatre paying, because, you know, dear Mrs. Lancaster, the railroads are sure to pay, and Richard knows everything about them," Amelia would say, lifting her large and rather inexpressive grey eyes to Adelaide's. "Everybody has such confidence in Richard. Papa says he is quite as clever about railroads as Mr. Hudson. Papa did not like railroads till he knew Richard—he was afraid they would encourage the Chartists; but now Richard has explained it all to him, and he has put ever so much money into them. Papa says Richard is clever enough for *anything*—he thinks he might be lord chancellor some day, if he were not so much taken up with railroads. But Mr. Bingham laughs at papa for saying that. He has just been made Mr. Justice Bingham, you know. But even he says that Richard is clever."

Mr. Vincent's little godchild was old enough to run alone when Amelia came on her second visit, and Amelia's own little girl was six months old. Vincent had taken a house in Bloomsbury Square, when he married. He was now secretary to the Cloppingford Junction Railway, and a director of several lines not yet begun, but the Bills for which he was helping to push through before the end of the session.

"I wish poor Mr. Lancaster was as lucky as you are, Richard," said Amelia, one night, as she was unpinning the pale soft tresses of hair which were her chief attraction.

"What makes you think Horace unlucky, my dear?" asked Vincent, looking up from a letter he was writing on the broad window-sill of their bedroom.

"I don't know that he is unlucky, exactly; but he is not like you—you seem never to have any trouble with what you undertake, but poor Mr. Lancaster seems to be so worried about things."

"I am very often worried, my dear, far more, I should say, than Horace ever is."

"Are you really, Richard? I thought you could do *any*thing you chose."

"I wish I could, my dear," said Vincent, as he glanced over what he had written, and carefully folded it. "I find many things very difficult of attainment—a little success is easily got, but such success as would satisfy an ambition worth the name, constantly eludes the hand stretched to grasp it. A man thinks over and over again that he is safely planted on Fortune's ladder, and again and again the rung gives way under his feet, and he is left a mark for the scoffs of more fortunate climbers."

" They must be very ill-natured, I am sure, to scoff," said Amelia, who did not fully understand her husband's figure of speech. " But surely, Richard, you are doing very well now ? I'm sure the gentlemen who call to see you all seem as though no one but you would do for them."

" I perceive a possibility of fortune in the future, but my position is by no means assured as yet," said Vincent, who had put away his letter without addressing it. " By-the-bye, Amelia, I hope you will oblige me by not trumpeting my praises quite so loud as I heard you doing this afternoon. I appreciate the affection which leads you to do it, but it is in bad taste, and it may injure me in ways which you are unable to understand. It will do me no good for it to be supposed that I am neglecting my profession for speculation in the share market."

"I am very sorry, Richard. I should not have said so much about the gentlemen who come to consult you, if I had not wanted to give Mrs. Lancaster a hint to make her husband trust more of his money to you, as you said he was so timid about railroads; and I'm sure this play that Mr. Kiddle does not seem to like, will cost a great deal."

"My dear Amelia," said Vincent, patting his wife on the shoulder, "your little head is full of schemes for the good of everybody, but you cannot possibly understand the intricacies of the transactions between Horace and myself, and even if you did, nothing would do me more harm than for it to be supposed that I had made use of you to influence him in the investment of his moneys. Remember this, Amelia, and trust me to know what will best serve Horace's interests and my own."

"I'm sure, Richard, you know best about everything," cried Amelia. "But you must own that it is a great pity Mr. Lancaster is so obstinate. I suppose it is because he is a genius."

Horace scarcely deserved this charge. All things considered, he had yielded a great many points to his numerous advisers, most of whom preached a naked and undisguised expediency. Theodore Paston alone (of the men) recommended a bolder course.

"You are altogether wrong," he had said many times, when Horace complained of hope deferred. "You have been long enough in the provinces, and you will never do more than you have already done, if you stay twenty years. Your English provincial audience cares only for an actor who struts and rants—your own style is deteriorating insensibly under the applause of the shop and the ship-yard. Take a small London theatre—you have money enough—and there carry out your own ideas. Here you are lost; in London, there will be found enough people worth playing to to fill a small house. Your expenses will be less than they are here. It will be better, every way."

Vincent, however, took Kiddle's view—that a longer provincial experience was advisable, before facing the ordeal of a London audience. " He ain't even made the most of his time, sir, if you'll excuse the liberty of saying so," Kiddle had observed confidentially to Mr. Vincent. " When he ought to be making himself master of the details of the profession, he's grudging every minute that he's away from those plays he's writing, which, between you and me, sir, will be a dead failure. They're too high-flown for modern taste ; there's too much of 'em all round. Mr. Lancaster ain't not to say got his foot in the profession yet—not what I call getting your foot in. He might have done, but he ain't. Why, I picked up more about the general business in six months, than he has in four or five years. But then, bless you, I wasn't writing plays all the time, instead of looking about me."

" I have advised Mr. Lancaster to remain here another year, at the least," said Vincent, who always conveyed the impression that he agreed with Kiddle, but that delicacy to his friend prevented his saying so.

"For a gentleman that doesn't go in particular for the drama, you have an uncommon good notion of the thing, sir. I wish Mr. Lancaster would listen to you a little more. Perhaps you could drop him a hint about getting some new talent. I've broached the subject, but Mr. Lancaster didn't jump at it as I could have wished."

Mr. Kiddle here touched on a sore point. It had been becoming evident for some time that the public could only be attracted by a constant succession of novelties. The appearance of a travelling circus, a menagerie, or a company of strolling jugglers, would half empty the theatre. Lately, this had happened so often, that the manager had submitted, with a bitter pang, to the indignity of himself engaging some of these wandering *artistes*, and bringing them on by way of after-piece—with the effect of crowding the house with half-prices.

" They do not care to give an extra eighteen-pence to come in time to see the play," he said to Adelaide. " I did not abandon my profession to become a circus manager—I am very little better ! "

" Let us go to London, Horace, and have a little theatre, as Mr. Paston advises, and bring out all your own plays," said Adelaide.

" I believe you are right. The *Globe* was but a small theatre," said Horace, thoughtfully, his eyes straying towards the mirror which hung above Adelaide's head.

The efforts of the manager were encouraged as warmly as ever by the *Post;* but Theodore Paston made no secret of his contempt for pit, gallery, and boxes alike, and only continued to lead the band out of friendship for the manager. Horace had often begged him not to remain to the injury of his career, but Theodore refused to go.

" I am young," he said. " And I am learn-ing much, even here ; and I am writing my opera, without the temptation to finish in too much haste, which would certainly assail me the moment I left these pigs of ship-builders. And I am here among friends. I shall not go."

Theodore looked at Charlotte as he said this, but she only said, rather stiffly, that Horace had never expected Mr. Paston to remain very long in a position so much beneath his powers.

"You are sarcastic and unkind, Miss Charlotte!" cried Theodore. "But when my opera is finished, perhaps you will cease to despise me."

"I do not despise you, Mr. Paston, and I am not clever enough to be sarcastic. Addy, I'm going up into the nursery. Good morning, Mr. Paston. Your opera won't be finished yet, if you spend all your mornings in talking to us."

Charlotte marched out of the room, and was presently heard singing to the old piano up in the nursery.

"Miss Charlotte is offended with me—her manner is quite changed," said Theodore, after listening in silence for a few minutes.

Horace was standing at one of the windows, making notes in his pocket-book, and had not observed this passage between Theodore and his sister. "Offended! Why, Mr. Paston, it is you who must be changed, to fancy it," said Adelaide, laughing. "You are grown quite suspicious. Charlotte, who is so good-natured to every one!"

"She was once kind, but she has long been so cold that I am sure I have offended her," persisted Theodore, pulling at his long hair till he looked like the "wild German musician" Lady Overton called him.

Theodore did not tell Adelaide the precise date of Charlotte's change of manner towards him, but he was persuaded that ever since Adelaide's marriage, Charlotte had become unaccountably haughty and inaccessible. Theodore was no vainer than most men—indeed, he was perhaps a little less so than most *artistes;* but he had once imagined that Charlotte looked on him with favour, and he was therefore much surprised to find that she now

took every opportunity of snubbing him. He
had read the *Elective Affinities*, and believed
that he thoroughly understood female human
nature. For instance, he had always understood Adelaide; but Charlotte baffled and
puzzled him sadly.

"Just listen to this; I am going to insert
it in the *Post*," said Horace, turning over a
leaf in his note-book. "'Mr. Lancaster is
sorry to announce that, in consequence of the
insufficient support he has met with, he will
be compelled to close the theatre at the end of
this month, the receipts not having covered
one half of the expense incurred in the new
scenery, etc.' We cannot possibly go on like
this," continued Horace, as he tore out the
leaves on which this announcement was written.
"Kiddle says there was not ten pounds in
the house last night, including the boxes. I
am determined not to go on filling the house
with paper—it is unworthy the dignity of the
drama. If there are not better houses, I will
go to London at once."

The immediate effect of the announcement was a great improvement. The Dockhampton people had become aware that the manager of their theatre was being praised in the London papers for his efforts to raise the English drama, and they were shamed into patronizing him. But in a month or two, the attendance began to fall off once more; and Kiddle renewed his persuasions that the manager would enlarge his company, and no longer rely chiefly on his own dramatic reputation.

" You must give 'em something new," said Kiddle. " The same people come over and over again. It's not as it is in London, where you get a fresh lot every night of your life, and they will have novelty."

Rather to Kiddle's surprise, Horace yielded. Perhaps, however, his motives for so doing would not have satisfied the practical second-in-command, had he known them. They were much the same as those which had decided him to remain for the present in Dockhampton. He shrewdly reflected that he would

probably have more leisure even here for the
completion of his unfinished plays, than
amidst the labours and anxieties of a new
venture. While with regard to the engagement of at least one new actor who should rival
himself, the fact was that Horace did not care
for the parts afforded him by many of the
plays which he had of late been driven to
produce, in order to keep the theatre even
tolerably filled. He grudged the time given
to these parts, and did not even much care to
succeed in them. He was, therefore, not very
unwilling to leave them to some actor who
would not feel it to be a condescension to play
in *The Stranger* or *The Robber of the Rhine.*
Horace considered that his own duties would
thus be lightened, and he would be able to
give a less divided attention to the tragedies
from which he hoped to derive a double
immortality. When therefore Kiddle, who
had run up to town for the purpose (and who
came back much impressed by the improvements on the railroad), expatiated on the

merits of Mr. Willoughby, of the *Standard*
Theatre, Horace wrote to Vincent, now returned to London, and begged him to go and
judge for himself whether Willoughby was
likely to take in melodrama. " For to this
I am reduced, Dick, though but for a time.
Jugurtha is finished, and I am now at work
(in the intervals of base interruptions) on a
new play, the subject taken from Spanish
history."

To this Vincent replied, in due course, that
he had seen Willoughby, and thought he
would probably be acceptable to a public
which liked melodrama. " He has a good
voice, and he is evidently not afraid of his
audience," wrote Vincent. " He acts in an
artificial style, but good of its kind—a bad
kind, I am aware. You might do worse, and
could hardly do much better. I am sorry that
your apprenticeship is costing you so dear ;
but when I saw Willoughby's assured self-
possession, and contrasted it with what you
tell me of the nervousness you still occasion-

ally experience, I perceived the justice of Kiddle's arguments for your not coming to town just yet. You will be glad to hear that the Cloppingford Junction Bill has passed at last. Shares rose cent. per cent. immediately. I wish you had allowed me to buy in for you; but they are still comparatively low, so there is time to change your mind. I am extremely sorry for your decision about the other line I mentioned to you. The Bill will, to my certain knowledge, pass next session, if not this; and if you are to carry out the London scheme, you will be very glad to make up for your losses at Dockhampton. Even now, railway shares are as good as Consols—which, allow me to remind you, are subject to fluctuation."

Horace read this letter to Adelaide, who was rather indignant at the passage in which Vincent spoke of Horace's nervousness.

" No one would ever know it—except me— I can tell; but then I know how you feel always, Horace dear. Nobody else would know !" exclaimed Adelaide, warmly.

"The greatest actors on record confessed to stage fright," said Horace. "The more an actor feels his part, the more he fears that the audience may fail to understand it. However, I shall engage Willoughby."

CHAPTER XXVIII.

Is there confusion in the little isle?
The Lotus-Eaters.

MR. HILLYARD had never ceased to take a kindly interest in Horace and Adelaide, and he paid them a visit about the time that Mr. Willoughby was to make his first appearance at Dockhampton—just about which time, too, a second son was born to the manager. Adelaide was a little disappointed that her baby was a boy; but Mr. Hillyard consoled her by saying that it was better to have seven sons than seven daughters. "I've cleared out three of mine, to be sure, and Caroline's got a sweetheart now. But never you be sorry you've got a boy, my dear; he'll find a daughter for you some day, won't you, my fine fellow ? "

Here Mr. Hillyard transfixed baby's cheeks between his finger and thumb so dexterously, that the nurse was heard to remark that any-body might know he'd been a father. The little Horace, however, seeing that the baby's cheeks were pushed up into his eyes by this operation until he looked like an india-rubber doll, set up a dismal howl, and assaulted Mr. Hillyard with a nine-pin which he hap-pened to have by him.

" Here's a young cock that crows betimes," cried the delighted great-uncle. " I must find something for that youngster. Always stick up for your brother, my boy ! So Vincent ain't coming down again just yet ? Then I must go to him, that's all. Cousin Lancaster here says he knows more about railroads and shares and that sort o' thing than half the wiseacres on the Exchange. And I've got some money "—here Mr. Hillyard slapped a remarkably fat pocket in his check trousers—

"as I want to make into more; and I'd as soon take Vincent's advice about where to put it, as any man's I know. I've always had the greatest opinion of Vincent ever since he behaved so well about poor old Mr. Lancaster's will. That was a queer start, that was! And I never did see a young man take a thing so well—never! Well, it don't matter to him now. He's an M.P. and a railway secretary, and I don't know what; but 'twas plaguey hard on him then, and I never did see a young man take a thing so well—I never did!"

The new actor appeared first in *Virginius*— a part which Horace had long intended to play himself. Kiddle however persuaded him to let Willoughby " try and make a hit " with it. " A new play, with a new actor in the chief part—depend upon it, Mr. Lancaster, anything else will be a mistake. And you can play *Virginius* yourself afterwards. Why shouldn't you and Willoughby play *Virginius* and *Appius Claudius* alternate nights? It's been done in plays before now."

Horace declined to play *Appius Claudius*, which was given to A'Deane, whose peculiar mannerisms were less ridiculous than usual in his representation of the odious decemvir. Willoughby was a provincial star, with some small London reputation. He was not a gentleman—he signed himself "Tomkyns Willoughby," but Mr. Culpepper said that his name was Tomkins. Be this as it may, Willoughby could not compare with Horace in personal advantages. He was rather a small man—or appeared so, beside the manager. His movements wanted dignity, and his conception of a character never deviated from tradition. Both physically and mentally, he was less ponderous than Horace ; and when he was not stagey, he sometimes showed vigour of the commonplace sort. But his perfect self-possession on the stage was, perhaps, the circumstance to which he owed such success as he ever attained.

"I call it assurance," said Culpepper to Mr. Paston, with whom he had gradually

formed an acquaintanceship. "Impudence—
that's what it is; and that's what pleases
nowadays. Any one of our company can
act better than he can—even poor old
Larkin was a better actor; but he's never
flurried. He's always got all his wits about
him for the business, and the gallery likes
business better than acting. Good-looking?
I don't call him good-looking. An insig-
nificant little fellow, with a loud voice, and
impudence enough for anything—that's what
Willoughby is. And he gags in a way that
is perfectly disgusting. He spoiled me in
Icilius—regularly spoiled me. When I ought
to have come forward with *Virginia*, he
clawed hold of her hand, and left me like a
fool up against the pillar."

Mr. Willoughby was exceedingly well received in *Virginius*, and also in other parts
which he played. For a few weeks there
were very good houses, and Kiddle was tri-
umphant. But Horace felt that this prosperity
was bought at the price of his principles—

neither Willoughby's style of acting nor the
majority of the plays lately put on being
calculated to raise the tone of the drama to
the manager's standard. It was hard, too, to
see a decidedly second-rate actor received night
after night with an ovation at least as enthusiastic as that which had greeted his own
Hamlet. Horace, who had fondly dreamed
of composing tragedies while Willoughby
played in the *Lady of Lyons*, found himself
fidgeting and talking to Adelaide, when he
should have been lost in the sins and punish-
ment of Don Roderick. Charlotte was gone
to Oxford for a long visit to Dr. and Mrs.
Simpson, and Horace would hardly allow
his wife to spend half an hour in the
nursery.

"The children can do very well with
Susan," he said impatiently. "For Heaven's
sake, Adelaide, give me your attention! I
have asked you twice whether you think the
soliloquy too long."

Adelaide excused herself—she had fancied

she heard baby crying—and Horace began to
read the soliloquy again—

"'What is a curse but words? What words but empty
    air?
Mere pointless arrows, that may frighten babes ;
Not men—not kings.   Kings need fear nought but
    fear.
Shall I for fear of fear miss my desire?'

Adelaide," said Horace, breaking off abruptly,
"I have resolved to put on *Hamlet* on Friday,
and I will take the *King*."

Mr. Willoughby's *Hamlet*, though severely
criticized in the *Post* by the loyal Warrener,
drew longer than Horace's had done ; but this
was a mortification common to all actors, and
which brought some sort of consolation with it,
in the shape of larger receipts.   Other and
worse annoyances resulted from this revival of
Hamlet.   A'Deane was mortally offended at
having his great part taken from him.   He
was so obviously unfitted for *Polonius*, that he
was offered his choice of the *First Player*, the
Grave-digger, or the *Ghost*, and at first he

indignantly refused to play at all, talked about
his "arrears," and was leaving Kiddle's room
in high dudgeon. Kiddle, who did not want
the trouble of finding another actor at a
moment's notice, called him back, and dryly
observing that in Mr. Lancaster's theatre there
never were any arrears, asked A'Deane if he
had change for a "fi-pun' note," producing
that article from his cash-box as he spoke.

"Don't be a fool, A'Deane; you're well off
now, if you do play the *Ghost* or the *Grave-
digger* for once. The manager won't let you
play 'em both, as I wanted him. The *Ghost's*
a good part, and you've just got the voice to
suit it. Which'll you do ?—give me the change
out o' this, or take the *Ghost* ?"

Mr. A'Deane elected to swallow his wounded
feelings, and take the *Ghost*—perhaps assisted
towards this decision by the fact that he did
not happen to have change for a five-pound
note about him. His *Ghost* was very effective,
and frightened a young girl in the gallery so
much that she was carried out in hysterics.

Horace found it exceedingly difficult to put up with Mr. Willoughby's *Hamlet*. It must be owned that the new star was deficient in princely dignity. The *Post* said that in the scene with *Horatio* and *Marcellus*, his action reminded the spectator of a figure in the Lancers' Quadrille. But the pit and the gallery clapped lustily, and fairly shrieked with delight when *Hamlet* snapped his fingers under poor old *Polonius'* nose, as he exclaimed—

"Am I not i' the right, old Jephthah?"

It was but too evident that the Dockhampton play-goers appreciated Mr. Willoughby as an actor far more than Horace. They had been attracted by the novelty of the gentleman amateur, by his fine stage presence, and magnificent costumes; but as an actor he had made no real impression at all. When he thought—and they thought themselves—that they were applauding the actor, they were only applauding his stature and comeliness, and the splendour of his diamond buckles. No one

cares to go over and over again to see diamond
buckles, or even to see a very fine man. But
Willoughby's acting appealed to them. His
rant was comprehensible, and if he had not
Horace's dignity, dignity may become monotonous. That Willoughby's " business " was
often highly inappropriate, was not of so much
consequence in the eyes of his audience, as
that there was always plenty of it.

So great was Willoughby's success, that
Kiddle urgently entreated the manager to
bring him out in some other Shakesperian
parts. " I do believe it 'ud draw," said
Kiddle. " 'Pon my soul, I do. You've trained
'em to some extent, and I advise you to bring
him out in *Richard III.*—we've got some old
scenery that 'ud do very well, touched up a
bit."

With the advent of Mr. Willoughby into the
company, a great change had taken place in
that little community. There had been
quarrels before. Mr. Culpepper had sulked
on his own wrongs, and fumed on those of

Miss Annesley.   Miss Annesley had had words
with Mrs. Kiddle; Mr. A'Deane had on one
or two occasions talked of pistols.   Most of
the members of Mr. Lancaster's company had,
at one time or other, felt themselves to be
singularly aggrieved by somebody or other, and
had said so with varying degrees of heat,
according as their natural tempers were
choleric or mild.   But all these misunder-
standings had blown over, without doing much
damage, even to the lookers-on—who usually
suffer the most in quarrels, as neutrals do in
wars.   There had also been changes from
time to time; but Culpepper, A'Deane, and
Miss Annesley still remained of the original
company, and Miss Elton might now almost
rank with them in point of time.

It happened very unfortunately, that, just
before Willoughby's engagement began, Miss
Annesley had a violent quarrel with Mr. Culpepper, or Mr. Culpepper had a violent
quarrel with Miss Annesley—for opinions
were divided as to the origin of the affair.

If Miss Elton knew it, she kept her
friend's counsel; and as for good old Mrs.
Annesley, who always came to the theatre
with her daughter, and worked at an inter-
minable patchwork quilt, she assured Mrs.
Kiddle that she knew no more than the
babe unborn, and had always told Annabella
that she had treated Mr. Culpepper very
badly, and would come to repent it. " A
very elegant young man, my dear, and
reminds me of poor Mr. Annesley. Ah! he
little thought I should ever come to live in
such a place as this!" said the old lady,
glancing not without complacency round her
pretty little parlour. " So small, my dear,
after what I have been used to. Poor dear
Mr. Annesley! he was always a very clever
man, just like Annabella — she's his image.
But there, my dear, girls will have their way,
and I do assure you I know no more than
that canary—a mule it is, and sings beautiful
—what the quarrel is about, except that it's
something about his taking offence at some-

thing she did. But I tell them they like quarrelling, just for the pleasure of making it up again."

Everybody believed, and a good many knew, that Culpepper and Miss Annesley were actually engaged, and no one expected the coolness between them to last more than a week, at longest. But Mr. Willoughby had made his first appearance before the week was up; Mr. Willoughby was unmarried, and was a fascinating man with the ladies; Mr. Willoughby was the star of the hour, and Mr. Willoughby paid Miss Annesley marked attention from the first. He was not so tall as Mr. Culpepper, but he dressed elegantly, and if he were not actually handsome, he behaved as if he were, and he was generally considered so. The easy assurance which charmed the public, and maddened Mr. Culpepper, gave him an immense advantage over that gentleman, who when angry was usually disconcerted and flurried. His rival (for such Culpepper instantly suspected Willoughby to be) made himself agreeable to the old lady, and was invited to tea on the very afternoon on which Culpepper dropped in to make his own peace. Willoughby, whose second visit this was, patronized Culpepper, as if *he* were the stranger, and appeared entirely unconscious of the latter's black looks, and attempts to exchange a word with Miss Annesley in private—all of which, however, he defeated, as it seemed, accidentally.

"I rather enjoy a provincial audience, for a change," said Willoughby, in reply to Miss Annesley ; "it is so amusing. In fact, a provincial *troupe* is amusing altogether. But you do the thing very well here, considering."

"There are very few London managers who are either able or willing to do what Mr. Lancaster is doing here," broke in Culpepper, who felt at the moment that he forgave the manager for everything—even for the Doric tunic.

"He wants to revive the legitimate. Good idea, but needs first-rate talent, and is deuced

expensive. Lancaster is a superior man—
I saw that at once. He wants experience,
and he hasn't got much style yet, but I've
no doubt we shall get on very well together."

"Sir," began Mr. Culpepper, almost choked
with indignation ; but he saw Annabella's
eyes fixed admiringly on Willoughby, and he
could think of nothing to say, which should
be at once cutting and gentlemanly.

As for Willoughby, he dropped his eye-glass
from his eye (he was much more near-sighted
than Culpepper—or professed to be—and could
therefore ignore any number of scowls and
haughty glances), and said with a sigh that
however ardently one might be devoted to
one's profession, it could not make one insen-
sible to the charms of domestic bliss. As
he said this, Willoughby looked in the
direction of Mrs. Annesley's gold spectacles,
thus depriving Culpepper of even the poor
satisfaction of reproaching Annabella for
allowing this impudent fellow to pay her
compliments.

Mr. Kiddle's first idea was to bring out *Richard III.* on the occasion of the Queen's visit; but for several reasons it was afterwards determined to defer the production till the theatre should be re-opened in the autumn. Vincent and his wife came down from London, and Charlotte and Mrs. Simpson came from Oxford to see the grand doings, which were a good deal spoiled by the rain. However, this gave an opportunity for Mr. Mayor and the Aldermen, like so many Raleighs, to spread their crimson robes of office in the mud for the Queen to walk over to her barge.

Sophia was looking wonderfully well. She had grown stout, but even this hardly made her look any older; she was in high spirits at the prospect of removing to London, whither the doctor talked of coming in order to prosecute some researches at the British Museum. She took an early opportunity of informing herself as to the business relations between Vincent and Horace.

"You tell me nothing in your letters, child.

I don't care a fig to hear what plays they have at the theatre; and as for Mr. Paston, I am very sorry Horace has a person who is so likely to encourage him in his vagaries. I hope this new actor's being so popular will open Horace's eyes to his folly in thinking a gentleman can succeed on the stage."

"Horace is a far greater actor than Mr. Willoughby, mamma. You should read what the *Post* said; here is the extract in my work-basket. The *Post* says that Horace aims at a far higher standard of excellence——"

"I declare, Addy," said Sophia, whose *embonpoint* had not blunted her keenness, "you're every bit as mad as Horace! Higher standard, indeed! We go to the theatre to be amused, and, of course, no decent manager would produce an immoral play. But I want to talk to you about serious matters. I hear of Vincent, even at Oxford; it seems he is dabbling in railways on his own account. But I am not to be bamboozled; I read the debates, and I agree with Colonel Sibthorpe that railways are worse than civil wars. Of course, I don't mean that there should not be a few railways between the great cities; but there will soon be as many railroads as there are towns, and I want to know where the money's to come from? How much has Vincent got Horace to put into this ridiculous line that he is director of?"

"Do you mean the Cloppingford Branch Line, mamma? Mr. Vincent is secretary for that."

"Director or secretary, it's all the same. Horace is entirely in his hands, and you have never exerted your influence as you ought against him."

"I have advised Horace not to put more money into railroad shares than he could afford to lose, and he said he never meant to do so. But I shall never try to make him quarrel with Mr. Vincent, mamma, and it is useless for you to ask me."

"I never did ask you, Addy, and you are an undutiful child to say so. You think, because you are married, you know as much as your mother, but I know the world better than you do or ever will. You are your poor father all over. I'm sure it is very hard, after all my efforts! I'm thankful to think that the doctor is not carried away by all these new railroads. He is pestered with circulars every day of his life, but he never even reads them. He says Mr. Bolland desired him never to take the money out of the Bank of England. It seems Mr. Bolland was bitten himself when they tried the railroads before; I was in India then, and knew nothing about it, but thousands were ruined, I'm told, and so they will be again, and Horace too, if you let Vincent have his way."

END OF VOL. II.

LONDON: PRINTED BY WILLIAM CLOWES AND SONS, STAMFORD STREET
AND CHARING CROSS.